Blackfoot
Moonshine Rebellion
of 1892

The Indian War That Never Was

A Novel by
RON CARTER

Bookcraft
Salt Lake City, Utah

Apart from historical figures,
all characters in this book are fictitious,
and any resemblance to actual persons,
living or dead, is purely coincidental.

Library of Congress Catalog Card Number 98-74341
ISBN 1-57008-557-9

First Printing, 1998

Printed in the United States of America

Note to the Reader

Although this novel deals with historical figures, such as President Benjamin Harrison and the Blackfeet Indians, it does not necessarily portray the characters or events in a manner that is true to the historical record. Rather, it attempts to tell a clever and often humorous story that now and then draws upon history to further the plot.

"White man speak with forked tongue!"

In the sickly light of the midnight quarter moon hanging just above the mountain skyline, Lump turned his massive head toward Injun Charlie, who thrust his face forward until his nose was a scant three inches from Lump's huge, round, flat face. When the two men could faintly make out the head of the other in the near total blackness of the cool Idaho night, Injun Charlie slowly and solemnly nodded his head to confirm the wisdom.

"With forked tongue," he whispered in choppy English.

Lump turned and reached in the darkness for their two companions, grasping one in each gigantic hand, pulling them close enough that he could feel their breath on his face. "White man speak with forked tongue," he quietly repeated in broken English, bursting with pride that Injun Charlie had given approval to the only English words Lump had ever learned.

None of them, including Lump, knew what had inspired the remark. Sneaking up in the murky dark on two barges owned by white men, it was just something Lump thought ought to be said, so he said it. And as was the habit of those in the tiny village from

1

whence they all came, none of them took exception.

Standing an even seven feet tall and weighing four hundred pounds, Lump was beloved by all who knew him. Loving, gentle, companion and guardian of all the children in the village, he had never been known to intentionally harm a soul—if you discounted the few times he had hugged someone he loved into unconsciousness. Nor had he ever been violent, except for the single occasion when a giant grizzly bear charged one of the toddlers in the village, and Lump knocked the bear senseless with one smashing blow right between the eyes.

Straining against the vice grip of Lump, each of the men quietly whispered, "with forked tongue" and waited until Lump slowly released his hold on their shirtfronts and their feet settled back onto the rocky ground. They scrambled up beside Injun Charlie on the lip of the gentle rise overlooking the mighty Snake River, a broad, faintly discernible ribbon winding through the darkness one hundred yards down the slope in front of them.

For several seconds the only sound was the murmur of an errant breeze in the tall, mountain pines. The four men squinted and strained to see in the darkness, but the two big river barges tied to the Idaho shore remained invisible. They knew they were there, because Drinks Much had stumbled onto them by accident while fishing weeks ago.

At first Drinks Much had not mentioned it to anyone. After all, they were just two big, empty, unguarded barges tied tightly to the shore and covered with brush. Eight days ago, however, returning to the village after helping an old trapper friend work on a jug until two in the morning, Drinks Much was terrified when he glanced through the pines on the river bank and saw a firefly so huge he fell to his knees in fear and prayed the Great Spirit would deliver him. In the midst of his desperate pleadings he heard hoarse whispers in the silence of the June night and marvelled at the thought of a whispering firefly. He opened one squinty, watering eye to peek cautiously, and through the alcohol fog that befuddled his brain, watched the firefly stop in midair while the whispering continued.

Startled that one firefly could whisper in two voices, sometimes both at once, he opened both eyes and saw two lurking figures come and go as they loaded something from a rowboat onto the barges. He watched them finish the work then pick the firefly from the branch of a pine tree, get into their rowboat, turn it around, and row back towards the Montana shore. In the total darkness, Drinks Much puzzled over what he had seen before he crept away from the river.

The next morning he quietly snuck back to the spot in broad daylight and, when he was certain no one was around, crept down to the barges. He soon discovered where the two lurking figures had hung a lantern in a pine tree, and a few moments later Drinks Much boarded the nearest barge.

Of all the odors on the Idaho frontier in June of 1892, there was one on which Drinks Much was a leading authority. He recognized it when his old, worn moccasins hit the planking of the bottom of the barge. A slow smile split his face as he closed his eyes, let his head roll back, and savored the rank, acrid, cutting edge of the smell of pure grain alcohol.

The barges were three-quarters full of kegs of moonshine, so many he couldn't count them all. He trembled and licked his lips and wiped his mouth while he pondered what to do. For a blessed, fleeting moment he had visions of a heaven in which he hid on the barges and just stayed until he drank all the kegs dry, which his euphoric calculations suggested would take until late August. Overwhelmed beyond his own powers of plan or reason, he backed off the barge and slowly retreated up the mountain towards his tiny village, turning often to look back to where the barges were tied, to reassure himself he had really seen this impossible treasure.

Two nights later, well after midnight, he again watched the entire eerie procedure of the floating lantern while men loaded more barrels and kegs onto the barges in the dark. The next morning he snuck onto the barges to be certain it was true. He knew of the white man's law against Indians possessing moonshine, and knew he would have to be careful who he told.

He shook his head sadly at the thought of what had happened to the good old days. The Blackfeet had sat there in east-central Idaho, swapping furs and lies with the trappers, sharing moonshine and thinking they were in paradise. To the west, Chief Joseph of the Nez Perce tribe got into a jangle with the U.S. Cavalry at White Bird Hill and led them on a merry chase clear to the Canadian border before he gave up and came on back home to the Wallowa Valley. To the east, Sitting Bull and Crazy Horse of the Sioux got into a beef with that little banty rooster Custer and ran over the top of him one afternoon. To the south, Geronimo and Cochise of the Apaches were regularly beating up on the Sixth Cavalry and then leading them all over Arizona and New Mexico. To the north, the Bloods and Piegans sat there in Canada, coming south three times a year to steal moonshine and horses, and generally have enough fun to last until the next trip.

But no one ever heard much from the Blackfeet in all these goings on. They had no Sitting Bull, or Crazy Horse, or Geronimo, or Cochise, or Chief Joseph, nor did they want one. They just enjoyed sitting there in east-central Idaho in ignominious anonymity, trading and moonshining and watching everyone else run around getting shot at. So far as Drinks Much could remember, not one Blackfoot had ever painted or feathered up or carried a knife or gun in anger or even suggested they wanted to. Fathers and swappers and moonshiners they were; warriors they were not.

Fearful someone would soon be moving the fully loaded barges, Drinks Much finally decided he could share his secret with three others.

Injun Charlie. Born fifty summers ago, he was quiet, inquisitive, unassuming, stolid, wise, a thinker. His long, thin face was divided by a huge hooked nose that separated two beady eyes, giving him the appearance of an eagle. Hours after his birth, his mother looked out the teepee flap and the first thing she noticed, which by Indian custom dictated what she should name the newborn, was a wolverine slinking in the timber at the edge of camp. So she named him Wolverine, which in the Blackfoot tongue is Ferocious Cat that is Striped, because the wolverine is a mean cuss and has a light stripe running down the dark brown fur on each side.

But when the white trappers came in, they listened to his name and to them, it translated out something like, Striped Cat That Is Angry, which could be either a wolverine or a skunk. So with wry humor, for twenty years they called him Skunk. That worked unil Injun Charlie found out what Skunk meant and he changed his own name.

Drinks Much had shared most everything with Injun Charlie, from earliest memory. He remembered the deep talks they had over flickering campfires while Charlie puzzled over what to do about being called Skunk. Charlie had stared into the firelight and reviewed every Indian name they could remember, shaking his head sadly over how so many of them turned out to be something other than what their loving mothers intended.

Take Sitting Bull, the great war chief, for instance, Charlie had said. His mama looked out the teepee flap when he was born and saw an old, toothless bull elk lying on a rise east of camp, and named her newborn Bull Elk That Lies on the Rise. When the mountain men and trappers heard it, they puzzled on the translation, and it came out Bull That Sits on the Rise, which got shortened to Sitting Bull. The problem was, no one in the history of the world ever saw a bull sit, because bulls and cows can't. They drop their front quarters first when they lay down, and raise them last when they get up, and are never in a sitting position. Notwithstanding the case against bulls ever sitting, the name Sitting Bull stuck with the great Sioux chief all his life.

And old Charlie had shook his head when he talked about Crazy Horse. What really happened, he had quietly explained to Drinks Much over the campfire, is that the day Crazy Horse was born in August, it was hot and sweltery, and outside the teepee an old U-necked, spavined camp horse was dozing in the oppressive stifle of the late afternoon heat when a horse fly about two inches long snuck up under his tail to where the pucker starts and stung him for all he was worth. The frantic horse exploded, his screams echoing for miles as he tried to reach up under his tail to dislodge the stubborn horsefly. The horse went through gyrations unknown to horses until that day, trying to reach the horsefly with any hoof he could, then tried his teeth. The midwife who had just delivered the squirming new baby boy quickly jerked the teepee flap aside to see the uproar, and the new mother's eyes bugged out when she saw the screaming, acrobatic horse. In stunned amazement she said something that translates roughly, "Holy mackerel, would you look at that crazy horse?" And the baby was named.

Drinks Much grinned at the memory, and then his thoughts moved on to the other two people he trusted enough to include in his great, glorious secret.

Mole. Drinks Much would have to tell Mole because someone had to sneak up on those barges in the dark and be sure no one was on watch. And no one in the Blackfoot nation could sneak like Mole, who was as diminutive as Lump was huge.

Lump. Lump weighed eighteen pounds at birth and was born breach, which left his head peaked until he was three. At his birth, his relieved mother looked outside the teepeee and the first thing she saw was the mountain east of the village, so she named him Mountain. When the white men translated that, it could mean mountain, or projection, or hillock, or lump, so he became Lump. Drinks Much figured he would have to include Lump because if they got onto the barges they would have to have someone strong enough to lift those kegs. Maybe one hundred of them were at least fifty gallons, and the rest of them—maybe fifteen hundred—were five and ten gallons.

So Drinks Much called the three of them together in a secret place and explained what he had found and that he intended sneaking down there one night to test that moonshine to be sure it was good quality, then take about six barrels ashore. No one would miss just six barrels. And anyway, that would be just about the right price for letting those Montana moonshiners tie up their barges on the Idaho side of the river. If any trouble developed they would jump off the barges and disappear into the darkness.

When he finished explaining his plan they were all sitting there in the heat of the afternoon sun, wiping their mouths, licking their lips, eyes pleading. They instantly decided tonight would be just fine for liberating some of that moonshine.

So under cover of the black night, they snuck down to the barges. Drinks Much nudged Charlie and Charlie tapped Mole on the head and pointed him down the slope. In one second Mole had disappeared, to return five minutes later and report.

Four white men were guarding the barges, three

of them plumb unconscious from sampling the moonshine. To be certain, he had pinched their noses closed and held them until they started snoring through their mouths. The fourth man had drunk no moonshine and was sleeping lightly. He had to be put into a deeper sleep if they figured to get six barrels of the coveted moonshine.

Injun Charlie nodded and turned to Lump, whispering quietly. "One white man on barges unfriendly. Will hurt us. Maybe hurt children in the village."

Instantly Lump sat bolt upright in outrage and started to rise, intent on whomping the man who might be a threat to the children.

Injun Charlie grasped his arm. "Not hurt children bad. Just a little. So, not hurt him bad. Just one light whomp on head with fist."

Lump nodded his understanding and flexed his fist in anticipation. Injun Charlie concluded Lump was ready, and on his signal, three of them slipped over the lip of the rise and silently started sneaking down the incline to the barges. Lump lumbered along behind because it was impossible for him to slip over anything or sneak anywhere.

Silently, Mole led them to the tie ropes that bound the barges together and anchored them to the shore. He signed with his hands and pointed to where the fourth man was snoozing, and Injun Charlie signed to Lump. Eyes glistening with importance, Lump walked towards the barge, the earth vibrating slightly with every firm stride.

The guard on board snapped awake while Lump was still ten feet away and turned, eyes probing the darkness on shore. Dimly he saw the great shape moving in the murky blackness, but relaxed when he thought it must be a bull moose. Too late he remembered mooses don't wander around much at night and reached for his Remington. Lump's fist thumped him once lightly on the top of his head, and the man sighed and peacefully crumpled to the bottom of the barge, gone until at least sunrise. Maybe sunset.

Proud of his work, Lump reached over the side of the barge to be sure the man was asleep, and recoiled in utter terror. He felt the man's ears and nose, but above them, where hair should have been, was nothing but smooth skin. Lump had never seen a bald-headed man, and meeting his first one by feel in the dark caused him to rear bolt upright and back away in shock.

Instantly Mole jumped into the barge to find out what had scared Lump, and it took him ten seconds to figure it out and tell Injun Charlie.

Lump was backing up the hill when Injun Charlie called to him. "Nothing wrong. White man kind, generous. Loan hair to friend for two, three days."

Lump stopped, and his huge face finally broke out in a smile. Such an act of kindness he could accept. Then his mouth puckered for a moment before he asked, "Why warriors take scalps? Why warrior not just borrow hair for two, three days, feel like hero, then give hair back? No one get hurt. Much better." He looked hopeful.

Injun Charlie pondered that for a moment and realized he had no answer that would satisfy Lump, so he said, "Must get on barges, get moonshine. Talk about hair later."

A minute later all four men were on board the barge. Quickly, Drinks Much drew flint, steel, and tinder from his shirt and struck a tiny light, which he set on the head of a fifty-gallon barrel. Hand trembling, he signed Lump to break open the head of the next barrel to be sure it was moonshine.

In the flickering light, Lump misunderstood which barrel. His fist, about the size of the ham of an elk, smashed the one-inch oak boards of the barrel on which the tinder burned. Instantly the fumes of pure alcohol filled the air and the smouldering tinder was plunged into the volatile liquid. Flame leaped five hundred feet straight into the black-vaulted heavens, and for one terrified moment, all four men stood paralyzed, eyes wide and white, before the fifty-gallon barrel exploded like a volcano. Lump, Mole, and the bald-headed guard were all blown sixty feet back up the hillside, scorched and terrified, hair frizzed, but otherwise unhurt.

Then the chain reaction started. The barrels on either side ruptured, ignited, and blew, bursting the next barrels, and the most horrendous fireworks show in the history of the West was under way. The end of the barge was blown to smithereens and the mooring ropes shredded, setting both barges adrift in the river. In the process, Injun Charlie, Drinks Much, and the three drunk, sleeping guards were launched fifty yards out into the blackness of the Snake River. The shock of the cold water sobered the guards enough to stay afloat and swim for shore, where they, along with Drinks Much and Injun Charlie crawled out, stunned, bedraggled, sopping wet, and disoriented.

As the barges drifted towards the center of the river, the exploding fifty-gallon barrels began blowing the smaller five- and ten-gallon kegs stacked on top, hundreds of feet in the air, where they in turn exploded, splattering great showers of burning alcohol in beautiful patterns, hundreds of feet across, to light up the heavens and the surrounding country for two miles.

At Fort Lemhi, fifteen miles south, the Mormons who lived within the walls of the stockade all leaped from their beds and ran out into the parade ground, where they instantly began singing "Come, Come Ye Saints" and shouting "Judgment Day has finally come!"

Colonel Joshua Pape, commanding officer of the Fort Lemhi cavalry, spat orders to a sergeant who showed up barefoot and hitching a suspender over his shoulder. "The Indians have gone berserk, burning and looting! Get a patrol mounted instantly, reconnoiter, and report by dawn. If they ambush you, sell your lives dearly!"

Then Colonel Pape ordered the bugler to sound reveille, so the entire garrison could get armed and provisioned for a major campaign while the barefoot sergeant pondered whether he wanted to sell his life dearly or head home for Tennessee.

The Indians who had settled near the fort thought the army had begun another raid on the Blackfoot village, but they knew there weren't enough Indians over there to explain the gigantic fireworks display or the rumbling explosions. So they shrugged and gathered in a circle and danced the ghost dance while they enjoyed the unprecedented show.

Every human being within five miles of the barges was on the riverbank ten minutes after the first spectacular blast, eyes wide, not knowing what was exploding and burning, but absolutely mesmerized by the celestial fireworks display and the sight of what looked like the Snake River burning. Kids sat in family wagons, wrapped in blankets their parents had hastily thrown around them, and watched and oohhhed and ahhhhed with each new eruption.

Half an hour later, as the battered barges drifted into the current and sank lower in the water, more than eight hundred of the smaller kegs and sixty or so of the fifty-gallon barrels that had survived slowly floated free. Five minutes later they had been scattered by the current and were all over the river, drifting south.

Injun Charlie drifted a little ways downstream with the barrels, then began working towards shore, carefully pushing a ten-gallon keg ahead of him, until his feet touched bottom. He wedged the keg between two large rocks, jerked some cattails to cover it, and looked around for Drinks Much.

After a little calling, he located him and the two of them started walking back toward the crowd. They found Lump and Mole scorched black, but sitting among the onlookers on shore, spellbound by the show. Catching the general mood among the spectators, Injun Charlie benevolently fetched his ten-gallon keg and opened it. Four others were retrieved from the river and opened, and the crowd was soon in the finest mood of celebration and brotherly love those parts had ever known.

The cavalry patrol didn't report back to Fort

Lemhi until late afternoon the following day. The troopers were riding jaded horses, their uniforms muddy and splotched, each man riding slowly. They all held their heads perfectly still, eyes closed, occasionally pressing their temples with their fingers. The bugle blast announcing their return caused four of them to topple from their horses in sheer agony.

The Lieutenant slowly dismounted and tried to salute Colonel Pape as he made his report.

"Two barges of illegal alcoholic beverage burned by accident. There are about eight hundred barrels of the contraband floating down the Snake River. We recovered three, which we tested to be certain of their contents."

Pape's eyes bugged. "Eight hundred barrels of moonshine going to waste in the river?" He spun and shouted at the major standing three feet behind him. "We leave instantly! Forced march, full battle gear! Orders are to retrieve every barrel of that uh, um, er, medicinal alcohol from the river by any means necessary. We will hold it for a reasonable time so the owner can claim it. After that, we dispose of it."

The major snapped to attention. "Yes sir. What's a reasonable time, sir?"

"Twenty minutes."

"How do we dispose of it, sir?"

"Humphhh. Well, it's medicinal. Cures worms, warts, gout, and dysentery. How many in this command have worms, warts, gout, or dysentery?"

"Every last one of us, sir."

"Mount up!"

"For days the telegraph key at Fort Lemhi clattered, morning and night. From Leadore to the salt

14

water where the Columbia meets the Pacific Ocean, the word about the floating moonshine spread like wildfire, and everyone within ten miles of the river was shoving everything that would float into the water. They were using boats, tubs, crates, nets, pikes, fish lines, seines, grappling hooks, and log barriers to pluck the kegs from the river. Spontaneous celebrations sparked by medicinal alcohol became rampant all down the Snake and the Columbia at every town, settlement, hamlet, and camp. The Fourth of July celebration set all-time records for joviality and participation.

The last two fifty-gallon barrels were netted by a fishing trawler at the mouth of the Columbia. At his home port of Vancouver, Washington, the generous trawler captain shared his catch with the village, which slept not at all that night, so raucous did the celebrating become.

" That's the most ridiculous bunch of letters and reports I ever saw!"

United States President Benjamin Harrison tossed the sheaf of papers onto his desk in the oval office at 1600 Pennsylvania, Washington D. C., pursed his lips, and screwed his face into a prune. He scowled darkly as he jerked out of his chair and began to pace, hands clasped behind his pear-shaped frame.

"Part of them say we've got an Indian rebellion! Part says our cavalry massacred a bunch of those savages. One citizen claims he had a wholesale theft of half the medicinal alcohol west of the Mississippi! That idiot demands an investigation and restitution for all his losses!" His full beard wobbled with each word as his voice rose. "If he's dumb enough to keep medicinal alcohol out where someone can walk off with sixteen thousand gallons of it, then he's the one who gets to pay the bill when someone does it! Everybody's got their hand out!"

He paced towards the door, turned back and spat, "And that imbecile from the Department of the Interior! He says half the salmon migrating up the Columbia and Snake Rivers took three days off! Swimming in circles in small pools! Laying on the bottom! Attacking the grizzly bears who came to feed on them. What does he expect the President of the United States to do about salmon who don't know how to migrate? Set up a bureau to teach them?"

He stalked to the window, looking out onto a dreary, rain-soaked Pennsylvania Avenue and stood with his hands clasped behind his back, head thrust forward, mouth puckered, looking fierce.

"Humphhh," he forced through clenched teeth. "And on top of it, that donderhead Clarence Whittle walks in here unannounced and delivers his doomsday speech to me this morning. Stood right there dripping all over the government carpet."

Harrison's face dropped in consternation. "Better find a way to juice up your campaign, he says to me. Me! The President of the United States! If you don't find a way to sparkle, we'll find someone who can, he says."

Harrison jerked a handkerchief from his inside coat pocket and swabbed at a suddenly perspiring face. "How? The Civil War's over! The Indian wars are over with that fuss at Wounded Knee. I tried to make some claims in the International Courts against Samoa but no one in Congress cared because not one voter in this country had ever heard of Samoa."

He shook his head sadly. "I was even willing to start a war with Chile. Why, we could have whipped Chile with our ironclad navy in a week, but what did they do? They surrendered before I could give the orders. They may be a proud nation, but they had no choice but to apologize for their abuses."

He turned once more to gaze out at the overcast,

drizzly day. "I got Idaho and Wyoming ready for full statehood, but so what? Everyone knew that was going to happen."

He drew and exhaled a great, defeated breath. "So what am I supposed to do to sparkle, to dazzle the voters? Invade Canada? Send artillery down to shoot up Mexico?"

He threw up his hands in despair. "What kind of lousy fathers were Red Cloud and Sitting Bull! You'd think those two old buzzards would have taught at least a few of their kids how rotten we treated them and urged them to have enough spunk to stir up a bunch of young hot bloods to come shooting to get revenge. Lord knows they have reason enough to do it. And what's wrong with those Blackfeet? We stole their land and shoved them onto reservations and stuck their kids in white schools, and they just sit there. What does it take to get them mad enough to cook up a real resounding . . ."

He stopped cold in his tracks. His head jerked around, eyes wide with sudden inspiration. "That's it! By thunder, that's it!" He smacked one fist into the other palm and whipped around his desk, fingers trembling as he seized the official report while his fevered eyes went over every word.

"That's it! Genius. Sheer genius. The long-awaited Blackfoot Indian War. It has finally, at long last, providently erupted all up and down the Snake and Columbia Rivers. Beautiful! Glorious! Raiding, burning, plundering, destroying everything and anything needed by the settlers, and most particularly all their medicinal alcohol! The United States cavalry, gallantly plunging into the treacherous depths of the

18

Snake River to rescue the sixteen hundred barrels which were intended to save and comfort the lives of the brave and courageous pioneers and homesteaders. Perfect. Perfect!"

Eyes glowing like revived embers, he settled back into his chair and rubbed his hands together again and again, chuckling low to himself. "Now, how best to go about this." An hour later he whacked his fist down on the oval desk and shouted "I've got it! Orville, where are you? We've got work to do."

Orville Peabody, sporting four days of white whisker stubble, his bow tie off center and tied too loose, slouched into the rounded, superbly decorated room and stood by the desk. "Yeah, boss?"

Orville had become Harrison's personal secretary when Harrison was forced to pay a political debt. Orville's brother, Wilmer, was elected a senator from Colorado, and promised Harrison the Colorado electoral vote if Harrison would hire his brother into the White House. Harrison made the deal without seeing the brother.

Forty-two-year-old Orville had been a Nevada sheepherder the first twenty years of his life and a Colorado Rockies gold prospector, mule skinner, saloon swamper, and general wastrel the last twenty-two. He seldom wore his suit coat and bathed twice a month, at which time he also shaved.

By iron will, Harrison masked his disgust at the sight of Orville. His suitcoat was missing and his trousers had been uncleaned, unchanged, and unpressed for more than three months now. "Orville," Harrison said, "Have the head of the Bureau of Indian Affairs over here first thing in the morning. Eight o'clock. Then get the head of the War Department here by ten o'clock. Understand?"

"Sure, boss. Anything else?" Orville shifted his generous cud of tobacco from one cheek to the other and wiped the sleeve of his white shirt across the slight leakage at the corner of his mouth. He rubbed the tiny brown streak on the shirt sleeve onto the growing collection of stains on his trouser leg.

"No, that's all. Urgent. Get onto it."

"Right now, boss." Orville shuffled out of the room.

"Oh, and Orville, can you get a couple of much larger, nice-looking cuspidors, one for your office, one for mine?"

"Sure, boss. Why? I been missin' again?"

Harrison forced a wooden smile. "Only occasionally. You're improving."

Orville nodded and walked back to his office for his coat.

The next morning at eight o'clock sharp, Harrison answered the knock on the oval office door. "Come in."

Orville entered, a huge cuspidor locked under his arm. "I got the Indian Bureau guy here, boss," he said, and traded the huge cuspidor for the smaller one under the overhang of the great oval desk, near the president. With the spittoon in place, Orville could not resist. He unloaded one gigantic, juicy squirt, dead center in the opening. His eyes shined. "She'll do, boss," he said, and ran his sleeve over his mouth.

Harrison watched the performance with thinly

veiled disgust. "What is the name of the man from the Bureau of Indian Affairs?"

"Uh, Wally. Somethin' like that. Yeah. Wally Carp. That's it."

"Show him in," Harrison said through gritted teeth.

Orville grinned and shifted his cud. "Sure, boss." He ambled out, jerked a thumb over his shoulder and said, "Wally, he's waitin'."

Harrison beamed his best political smile and shook Carp's hand warmly. "Nice to see you again, Wallace. How are things with the missus and children?"

Carp stared blankly. "The missus died seven years ago. The kids are both grown and gone."

Harrison clacked his jaw shut for a startled moment. "Oh. Of course. How forgetful of me. I'm sorry about the missus. Now, Wallace, let me come directly to the point." He thrust his lower lip forward for a moment and looked presidential. "I have received some rather disturbing news about an incident on the Snake River in Idaho. Concerns some Blackfoot Indians and medicinal alcohol. Heard about it?"

"Yes. Nothing to it. Pure bunk."

Harrison smiled broadly. "Wonderful! That's what I like to hear. Right on top of the affairs within your bureau. By jove, that's what makes this government tick." He slowed and sobered. "There's just one thing. Do you think it would be a good idea to have someone, just anyone, go out there on the train and take a look personally and file a formal report? I would like that file closed with a final report. We got an election coming this November you know."

Carp settled back in his chair and studied Harrison. "Anyone in mind?"

Harrison shook his head grandly. "Oh, no, I trust your judgment implicitly. Anyone loose in your department right now? A secretary, a clerk, just anyone?"

Carp scratched his lean jaw. "Well, we have a new assistant clerk. Happens to work in the accounting department that keeps track of the rations we send to the Indian agencies out there. Got a memory that absorbs everything. Nice quiet guy. Maybe he . . ."

"Marvelous! Perfect! Just a quick trip out and back, to be sure everything's ship shape out there. What's his name?"

"Caleb Dinwoody. But I've got to warn you, he's never been west of Washington, D. C. Born and raised in Baltimore."

"Just right! Won't be missed much for a few days. Can you have him here by one o'clock today? I'll have to instruct him and give him my letter of authorization."

"He'll be here." Carp studied Harrison with a jaundiced, suspicious eye as he rose to leave. Harrison dropped his arm affectionately around Carp's shoulder and walked him to the door. "Let me know when Dinwoody gets back and you have his report. And give your missus and the kids my best regards."

Carp shook his head slightly in resignation. "Yeah, right, Mr. President. I'll be sure to do that."

As soon as the door closed behind Carp, Harrison jubilantly dropped into his chair, barely able to contain his elation. At ten o'clock sharp Orville walked in without announcement, followed by a stocky man who walked stiffly with his square jaw set and his close-cropped hair bristling.

"Boss, this here is Percy Bangmaker from the War Department. You ast for him to be here at ten o'clock."

"Bangmeister," the man said, irritated.

"Bangmaker, Bangmeister, whatever," Orville said, and shrugged.

"Thank you, Orville," Harrison said. "That will be all."

"Right, boss," Orville said. He could not resist. His head jerked slightly forward as he sent a perfect stream of brown tobacco juice into the cuspidor. He looked at Bangmeister condescendingly, wiped his stained shirt sleeve across his mouth and swaggered out the door.

"Have a seat," Harrison directed, and Bangmeister sat down, facing the oval desk. "Let me come directly to the point. We're in a state of war. The Blackfoot Confederation of Indians has risen in the bloodiest rebellion in the history of the West. A tragic, horrible thing. Have you heard about it?"

Bangmeister recoiled, and his face pinched down to a fine focus as he struggled. "I heard three or four peaceful Blackfeet tried to snitch some moonshine and accidentally set it on fire. About sixteen thousand gallons of contraband hooch got burned and dumped into the river. Gave the folks quite a show and stirred things up clear to the mouth of the Columbia. Turned out to be the best time those folks've had in ten years. Is that what you mean?"

Harrison reared back in utter shock. "The reports are clear! Burning, plunder, raiding—a full-scale Blackfoot uprising for a thousand miles. Troops from Fort Lemhi were mustered in the middle of the night and could not return for days. The settlers are living in a state of terrified, mortal fear! Why, one man, a Mr. Gideon Lumley, lost his life's work in one night."

"That the guy who owned the illegal moonshine?"

"Illegal, you say? Why, that man had invested his entire life's savings in preparing medicinal alcohol for the merciful work of tending and healing the wounds and illnesses of the brave pioneers who are settling the region. Everything he owned in this world was gone in one night of hideous Indian attack!"

Bangmeister leaned back in his chair, tipped his head back, and closed his eyes in disbelief.

Harrison plunged on. "So I am sending a secret agent, armed with my personal letter of authorization, to travel day and night until he has personally witnessed the atrocities. Then he will return and report. The moment we have that report you must be ready to send at least five regiments of the best cavalry and infantry you have, fully armed and provisioned, to restore order to our western frontier." Harrison straightened and waited.

Bangmeister stood and rubbed the back of his neck. "Let me get this straight. Four friendly Indians went to snitch some moonshine, accidentally set it on fire, and sixteen thousand gallons of it either burned or floated down the river. We got rid of two barge loads of illegal, contraband booze, everything's back to normal, and everybody out there had a great time. So why are we talking about five regiments of troops to restore order?"

Harrison reared to his full height. "You, sir, have jumped to a conclusion without seeing the actual reports I have on my desk, and certainly before you have seen the report of my secret agent. Until that information is made available to you, you would show better judgment by withholding any conclusions. In the meantime, you are under orders to prepare five regiments of your best men for battle."

Bangmeister shrugged. "You're the commanding officer. Who's leading the Indians?"

"Four Blackfoot war chiefs."

"What names?"

Harrison cleared his throat. "Ah, uh, . . . that is not clear."

Bangmeister stifled a grin. "My reports said they were Lump, Mole, Drinks Much, and Injun Charlie. I don't recall ever seeing those four names on anyone's roster of war chiefs."

"You will! Chief Lump is a monster of a man, a monster! You just prepare your troops to be ready to travel within ten days."

Bangmeister moved toward the door. "Yes, sir. They'll be ready." He walked back into the anteroom and looked at Orville. "Looks like we're getting ready for another election year."

Orville shook his head in wry sarcasm as Bangmeister walked out.

The minute the door closed behind Bangmeister, Harrison slumped into his chair, and all the air went out of him. He dabbed at the perspiration on his forehead. "Close," he murmured to himself. "Too close."

At one o'clock p.m. Orville walked through the door. "Boss, they's a fella out there name of Dinwoody. Caleb Dinwoody. Got sent here by Carp but ain't got no notion why. You know somethin' about this?" Orville cut loose with a dead-center shot at the spittoon and added to the collection of brown streaks on his sleeve.

Harrison straightened in his chair. "Send him in. That will be all."

Orville walked out, and a man walked in. Stooped slightly, he stood one inch short of six feet. He walked hesitantly, as though perpetually fearful of offending someone. His straight brown hair was parted down the middle, and his round, gold-rimmed glasses rode low on his nose, which he wrinkled continuously. He carried his bowler hat in his hand and kept his head tipped slightly back to keep his glasses from falling off.

Harrison sighed in relief. "Please have a seat, Mr. Dinwoody."

Dinwoody examined a chair, then carefully sat down on the leading edge, back ramrod straight, knees together, his bowler hat set squarely on his lap. With his head tipped back, he stared down his nose at Harrison and coughed a small, sickly, hacking cough.

"Dinwoody," Harrison said paternally, "I have a vacation sort of mission for you. All you have to do is travel west, take a quick look at some conditions there, and then skedaddle right back here and tell me about it. Shouldn't be out there more than one day. Wonderful chance to see this great country from the windows of a train, going and coming. Do you think you can do that?" Harrison smiled his most beguiling, political smile.

Dinwoody did not move. He just stared down his nose at Harrison, through his spectacles, in shock, and coughed a little cough.

"Don't forget yer suitcase, Sonny."

Dinwoody turned back towards the moving train just as the conductor tossed the suitcase out the door. It caught him full in the chest, knocked him two steps backwards, and fell skittering on the weathered, splintery planking of the depot platform. He recovered, reached for the suitcase, and jumped two feet sideways when the steam whistle on the locomotive cut loose, and the drive wheels on the giant engine suddenly engaged. They whipped out about twelve revolutions, slowed, and slowly started moving the train. The air-intake and steam-exhaust valves alternately sucked and blew, swallowing him momentarily in a cloud of steam.

POCATELLO, IDAHO, the sign on the squat, drab, mustard-colored building said. To his right, past the depot, fifteen or twenty clapboard and tar paper shacks straddled the tracks. To his left, a few tents and some more haphazard, off-plumb buildings stood at irregular intervals, none square with the next. Walking among the buildings in the late afternoon July sunshine were people of every description, dress, and language in the world, so far as Dinwoody could discern. Horses, mules, donkeys, jackasses, pigs, sheep, and chickens raised an insufferable din on every side as they squawled their displeasure at the world. The smells were as various, sharp, and pungent as the people and the animals and the sounds.

Hunched forward with his bowler hat clamped clear to his ears, head tipped slightly back so he could stare through his spectacles, Dinwoody walked slowly to the end of the platform. He descended the ramp into the dusty, rutted street and threaded his way through the confusion, intently reading the hand-scrawled signs on the building fronts. When he ran out of buildings he crossed the soot-covered railroad tracks and started back on the other side, squinting to read the building signs.

"Watch yerself!" The booming voice jolted Dinwoody to a jerky stop. "That there wheel mule can kick yer hat off without mussin' yer hair, and ol' Buttercup don't like strangers comin' up on her hindquarters that-a-way!"

Dinwoody stared at ol' Buttercup's hindquarters, a scant four feet from the end of his nose. He backed up and looked to see who had shouted the warning. The man held a tug chain in one hand and the hitch ring on a single tree in the other while he worked at unhitching a team of six mules from a gigantic freight wagon. The stubby, bearded, grizzled freighter seemed as broad as he was tall. Behind him, a taller, slender man worked at unhitching six more mules from a second freight wagon, as huge as the first.

Dinwoody swallowed and backed up two steps from ol' Buttercup. "Er, Sir, could you tell me where to find a hotel, if there is one? And perhaps the police?" The contained, sickly cough followed.

The man dropped the trace chain and placed one pudgy, powerful hand on the hip of the mule. "Hotel's that big tent right down there," he said, jerking his thumb over his shoulder without turning. "Ain't no police. Deppity U.S. Marshall's office is just past the hotel, right next to the Chinese laundry. Black tar paper building. But you can fergit lookin' for the law for a while. Marshall's in his own cell right now, sleepin' off about a gallon of moonshine. None of my business, but why you needin' the law anyway?"

"Oh, indeed I don't need the law, Sir," Dinwoody said hesitantly in his rather high tenor voice. "I thought a policeman might be able to give me directions."

"To where?" the squat man challenged. He knocked dust from his woolen pants that were stuffed into knee-high boots and held up by heavy suspenders. He wore no shirt; and his red, long-handled underwear lacked two buttons of covering his corpulent paunch.

Dinwoody's hand went to the breast of his suit-coat, where he removed the envelope from the inside pocket. "A place called the Settlement. Geographically I believe it is north of some place called Leadore."

The short man snorted so hard the mules flinched. "Pilgrim, you think you're going to the Settlement? Dressed like that?"

Dinwoody licked his parched lips and looked down at his rumpled suit, white shirt and bow tie, and black, high-topped button-up shoes. "This is not acceptable?" he asked, eyebrows raised in despair.

"Might be all right once you get there unless someone dies in a fit laughin' at it. But gettin' from here to there, them clothes don't stand a chance. You walk or you ride a mule or a horse, or you catch a lift on a freight wagon, and any one of them choices will go hard on them clothes. And any way you do it, it takes about fifteen days, dependin' on injuries, breakdowns, waterholes, rain, flood, drought, diarrhea, and varmints. Just warnin' you, Pilgrim. Good luck." He shoved his battered old black felt hat towards the back of his head and turned to his trace chains and single trees and mules.

"Thanks," mumbled Dinwoody, and he proceeded on up the street to the big tent with the word HOTEL printed on a piece of cardboard and nailed to the canvas front. He set his suitcase in front of the plank that rested on two barrels and served as a front desk. He timidly touched the bell stem.

"Hold on, I'm comin'," came a voice from behind a canvas drape that separated the sleeping quarters from the foyer. A moment later a skinny, hawknosed man parted the flap, and Dinwoody caught a glimpse of two rows of beds, reminiscent of a hospital. The man's head jerked forward and his face clouded as he sized up Dinwoody.

"What can I do for you?"

"I'm looking for some way to get up to the Settlement. I thought you might know how that could be done." He stifled a cough.

"Know where it is?"

"I have a map. United States War Department."

"Ain't no map I ever seen had the Settlement on it. But if you're goin' you best rent a horse or mule, and get some different clothes. Only other way is to walk or catch a ride on a freight wagon."

"No public transportation going north?"

The man leaned forward with his elbows resting on the plank desk. "Where you from, Mister?"

"Washington, D.C."

"Where's that? Oh, you mean the capital? Back East?"

Dinwoody nearly wept with joy at hearing the first word that connected his neat, orderly, beautiful world to the squalor of this one. "Yes. You've been there?"

"Nope. Just heard of it. There ain't no public transportation going north. Walk, ride something, or catch a freighter. Them's your choices. Now I got to go back and toss out a drunk or two and change some sheets." The man disappeared back through the drape.

Slowly, Dinwoody picked up his suitcase and walked back into the street, staring blankly, confused as he started aimlessly back towards the railroad station. As he passed the corner of the next building a pleasant, bright voice hailed him from behind.

"Mister, I hear you're looking for a ride north."

With hope flooding through his being, Dinwoody turned and waited while the man walked towards him, a smaller, silent companion following.

"Yes, I am."

"Well, now, it so happens we're leaving in the morning for a place called the Settlement. Driving a wagon. Just might have room for a passenger."

Dinwoody turned his face to the blue heavens, closed his eyes, and breathed a prayer of thanksgiving before he again faced the man. "What would the cost be?"

"Well, we'd have to work that out," the man said with a reassuring smile. "Come on back here and we'll show you the wagon and think about what it might be worth."

Gratefully Dinwoody fell in step with them and they marched to the rear of the building. Dinwoody stopped and looked about, puzzled.

"You mentioned a wagon? I don't see one."

"Oh, that," the man said, and turned to his companion. "Homer, would you go get the wagon?" Homer nodded and started back towards the street.

The man smiled grandly at Dinwoody. "He'll be back in a minute with the wagon. I thought it would be better if we discussed terms of the deal back here, off the street. Do you have money to pay your fare?"

"Yes. Right here." Dinwoody reached into his inside coat pocket for his wallet. The last sound he heard was a slight rustle from behind, and the last thing he saw was the smiling man take one step backwards.

One hour later Dinwoody timorously opened his left eye a very small slit and waited until he could force a focus. The snuffling sound near his head slowly materialized into a yellow cur dog that was sizing up Dinwoody's left ear. From the stench and the warm, wet feeling, he understood the dog had already sized up his left foot. In desperation he forced his hand to move and made a feeble pass toward the dog, which snarled and snapped. Dinwoody kicked with his wet foot and the dog slunk

33

off, pausing only long enough to vent its frustration by drenching the corner of the building before disappearing.

Dinwoody grimmaced at the pounding in his head and carefully explored it with his hand. He winced and groaned when he touched the huge knot where his bowler hat had been and gritted his teeth at the sharp stab that lighted the inside of his clenched eyes. Groaning, he raised on one elbow and tried to remember. "*I was talking to someone about going . . .*" His eyes flickered open and suddenly popped wide in shocked terror.

His clothes were gone! All that remained was his red, long-handled underwear and his glasses. He was laying in an alley, exposed for the world to see. Frantically he searched for his suitcase, which was nowhere to be seen. He tried to rise to one knee to hide, but was too unsteady on his legs.

He could absorb no more. It was not enough that he had come to the cesspool at the end of the earth. Now he was stripped to his underwear, in public, with his wallet, identification, money, and credentials gone, and no means of getting a stitch of clothing to cover himself. He resigned himself to his fate and lay down flat on his back, closed his eyes, placed his arms across his chest, and said aloud, "Dear Father, would you please receive your humble servant back into they presence? Instanter?"

"What you mumblin' about, Pilgrim?"

Dinwoody jumped half out of his underwear and both eyes popped wide while he frantically searched the heavens to see from whence God had spoken.

"You havin' trouble?" came the raspy, bellowy

voice, and Dinwoody clamped his eyes closed, paralyzed with the prospect of meeting God face to face.

The squatty, square mule driver walked from the corner of the building. Dinwoody heard the footsteps and cautiously opened one eye, then the other.

"You sure got peculiar notions," the voice continued. The beard was split by a grin, followed by a belly laugh.

Dinwoody relaxed. "I am praying to God to take me. I'm finished." He hacked his small cough.

"Horse pucky. You ain't hardly begun. The Settlement is a long way north. I see you started to get some new clothes, but why'd you stop with just gettin' rid of the old ones?" The laughter was uproarious.

Dinwwody waited until the man quieted. "I didn't. I've been robbed. Clothes, money, everything."

"That's what I figgered. I seen your little chamber pot of a hat walkin' up the street about twenty minutes ago and it didn't take long to figger it out. Want 'em back?"

Still lying full length in the dirt, Dinwoody quietly said yes.

"Okay. Get up off your backside and let's go get 'em."

In the gathering dusk the man grabbed Dinwoody by the back of his underwear and, in one heave, set him on his feet. Dinwoody gasped at the power he felt in those stubby, sinewed arms. He followed as the man strode purposefully out to the street, and suddenly Dinwoody remembered he was barefoot, in his underwear. A few people glanced at him but paid no attention as they hurried about their

35

business. Dinwoody sucked his lungs full of air, threw out his chest, and marched across the street as though he walked about in his underwear all the time. He followed the man past a weathered, unpainted, tumble-down building inside which a tin-pan piano whanged, and loud, raucous talk and laughter spilled out into the early evening. The man paused in the alley, looked around until he found a pick handle, and then walked directly to the rickety rear door of the old ramshackle building.

He spit on both hands, grasped the pick handle, and turned to Dinwoody. "Here we go," he said firmly. "Once we open the dance, yer on yer own. When the battle starts, hit them, not me." He raised one foot, kicked the door off its hinges, and plunged into the room. Horrified, Dinwoody hesitated for one full second, then closed both eyes and plunged in after him.

Inside, four men instantly turned their heads towards the door and froze. They were huddled around a table that was loaded with playing cards, money, poker chips, whiskey glasses, and two half-empty bottles. Cigar smoke hung heavy under a kerosene lamp on a wire above the table. The man nearest the door was wearing Dinwoody's expensive. Fifth Avenue bowler hat. He jumped up instantly and bolted for the door.

The squatty man swung the pick handle with both hands and the man in the bowler hat hit the floor in one corner and did not move. The man wearing Dinwoody's black suit coat tried to rise, but the squatty man caught him with the backstroke of the pick handle and he stopped rolling in another corner.

Dinwoody stood stock still, memsmerized by the sudden, furious battle, unable to move, and when the third man, who was wearing Dinwoody's shoes, tried for the door, he ran headlong into the frozen Dinwoody and they went down in a heap. Before either could rise, the pick handle had struck again, and Dinwoody's shoes were saved. The last man nearly made it past them before the squatty man threw the pick handle, which struck the fleeing culprit in the back of his head. He was four feet out the door before he quit rolling.

The squatty man sucked in his belly and snuffed a big snuff and said, "Well, I figger we got back most of your stuff. That your suitcase under the table?"

Dinwoody was paralyzed. His eyes were glassy. He was not breathing.

"Pilgrim, is that your suitcase?"

Dinwoody nodded hs head slightly and coughed.

"Okay. Let's git your clothes and money." He dropped to one knee and jerked the shoes off one man, and was working Dinwoody's pants and coat off another when he glanced at Dinwoody. He was standing bolt upright and had not moved.

"Pilgrim, you died of a stroke or somethin'? These here is your clothes, not mine. Git busy."

Dinwoody blinked his eyes and shook his head, and started towards his suitcase as the squatty man jerked the shirt off one of the unconscious men on the floor. The man stirred, groaned, tried to sit up, and fell back. He looked at who had just removed Dinwoody's shirt.

"Goldang you, Stump, you didn't have to hit so hard. You like to of kilt me."

"You mean I didn't? I figgered I had."

"That was just plain mean. Ornery. You could of asked." He struggled to make the world stop whirling and tried to rise to one knee.

"Did you ask the Pilgrim when you whomped him and stolt it all from him?"

"Naw, I guess yer right. Did you kill Harley or Pot? Where's Clarence?"

"They're all breathin'. Clarence's outside."

"Well, anyway, you didn't have no call to bust us with a pick handle."

"Maybe that was a little rough," conceded Stump. "Here, Stretch, hold still whilst I take a look." With a tenderness that surprised Dinwoody, Stump parted the hair around the lump.

"I don't think nothin' is broke. Here, wait a minute." Stump quickly shuffled through the mess on the floor and located a whiskey bottle with a little left in it. He parted the hair again and poured half the whiskey on the knob and rubbed it in before he handed the bottle to Stretch.

"Take a snort or two. And next time, you remember that this here Pilgrim"—he jerked a thumb towards Dinwoody—"is my new muleskinner. You want to go funnin' some newly arrived innocent, you make sure it ain't him. You hear?"

"I hear. I hear."

"Tell Pot and Harley and Clarence when they come around."

"I will."

Stump turned to Dinwoody. "How much money did you have when you come to town," he asked.

"Two hundred dollars."

Stump gathered bills from the floor, counted two hundred dollars, and threw the rest back down. He gathered up all the clothes, turned to Dinwoody, who had the suitcase, and said, "Come on." Dinwoody followed him outside, where they picked Dinwoody's wallet from Clarence's hip pocket and started for the street, Dinwoody walking gingerly in his bare feet.

Dinwoody cleared his throat. "What's a mule-skinner?"

Stump ignored the question. "What's your name, Pilgrim?"

"Dinwoody."

Even in the late dusk, Dinwoody saw the stark shock bordering on terror in Stump's eyes.

"*Dinwoody*," he spat. His eyes flicked up and down the street. "Don't you ever say that out loud around here again until you can whip a grizzly bear, because that's just what you'll have to do. A man has got to have a name that says something out here, and what *Dinwoody* says would be pure suicide. So you're Trace. A trace is a chain used to hook up a team to a wagon and it's a real important part, and it's tough. So you're Trace. Understand?"

Dinwoody nodded his head and again asked, "What's a muleskinner?"

"That's a man that drives a string of mules while they pull a wagon. I got to have three muleskinners to drive my three freight wagons north at dawn tomorrow, and I ain't got three. I only got Gimp and me. Buckshot run off with some scarlet woman from the saloon and won't be back until he's spent all his wages, and I can't wait. So you're my new mule-skinner. You wanted to go to the settlement, and that's where I'm headed. You get starters wages, which is two dollars a day and three meals."

"I never seen a mule in my life, before today."

"Well, these mules ain't seen you before today neither, Trace, so you start out even. Going to be dang interestin' to see which is the smartest. Now come on, we got to get over to the drygoods store before old man Tingey gets too far asleep, and we got to get you some genuine muleskinnin' clothes."

"Trace, you listen close because we ain't got time to do this twice. The long ears on these critters is on the end that bites, and the tail is on the end that kicks, which is also where the processed oats comes out. A mule that's been practicin' can kick a mosquito out of the air with either hind foot at six yards. So first lesson, get it straight which end you're workin' on and be ready for them to try to kill you."

Shoulders hunched as always, squinting through his spectacles in the gray predawn light, Trace nodded and moved one foot. "I feel real dumb in these clothes." He glanced down at his long-sleeved, gray hickory shirt, woolen pants held up by a broad, two-inch belt, and heavy suspenders. His trousers were tucked inside black, flat-heeled boots that reached to his knees, with the pulls dangling six inches from both sides of each boot. A black, broad-brimmed, high-crowned Stetson hat sat squarely on his head.

Stump shook his head in disgust."Fergit yer dang clothes. You look fine. If you'da showed up here wearin' them clothes from yesterday, we'da had a mule stampede clean to the Missouri. Now listen. Second lesson. You got to learn their names, because mules know their names and they're real finicky about it, and will sulk for two days if you call it wrong. First two here is Buttercup and Daisy. Second two is Bess and Belle. Third two is Zeke and Zeb. Got all that?"

Trace pointed and mouthed the names to himself. "I got it. How do you tell boy mules from girl mules?" He coughed his sickly, hacky cough.

"In mules there ain't no girls or boys. There's just mules. They can't have no offspring."

Trace's jaw dropped and he backed off one step to consider the sorry, heartbreaking plight of the mule for a moment.

"All right," Stump continued, "third lesson. You got to learn to beller. That don't mean talk loud or yell. That means beller like a buffalo with a belly ache. Now let me hear you beller."

"What do I bellow?"

"Anything you feel like."

Trace shrugged and said loudly, "Help!"

Stump winced in deep pain. "You ain't teachin' no Sunday school class. Lord, that wouldn't wake up the sleepers on the first row. BELLER! Listen."

Stump threw back his head and bellered "MULE," and thirty-six mule ears jerked erect, small wisps of dust raised from the ground, and dogs in town crawled under the porches. "See? Beller! Now try 'er again."

Trace looked both ways to be sure no one but Gimp and Stump were there, tipped back his head, and in a mild yell cried, "HELP!"

Stump shook his head. "We got to work on yer beller. Now, next lesson. You got to learn to talk Mule. You got to learn to shout things like, 'You lop-eared heathens', "you ornery beggars', 'You slab-sided coyote baits,' 'You ignorant gentiles.' And you got to shout 'em like you're just one step short of whackin' 'em with a pick handle, 'cause they think yer heapin' love and affection on 'em when you do. All right, try it."

Trace cleared his throat. "You lop-eared heathens. You ornery beggars. You slab-sided . . ."

Stump shook his head. "Shout, don't whisper. And you got to get more natural feelin' to it. Mules don't know you love 'em unless you learn to cuss 'em real loud in Mule. So we got to work on your Mule, too, besides your beller."

He grasped the thick, eight-foot hickory handle of a bullwhackers whip from the nearest loaded wagon and with an expert flick, the twenty-foot braided rawhide whip laid out in a straight line behind him.

"Now, last thing for this mornin', you got to learn how to use this here whip." He pointed. "See that horsefly over there on that waterin' trough?" With a quick twist of his thick wrists the rawhide whip snaked out like lightning and the horsefly, twenty feet distant, disappeared in a crack like a pistol shot.

Trace stared and swallowed.

Stump coiled the whip. "The whole idee of this whip is to make it pop over their heads so they think what that would feel like if it whacked 'em on the rump. Makes 'em pull real good. So you got to learn to make 'er pop good."

Trace nodded. "How do I make the mules turn right or left?"

"Don't worry none about that for now. I'll teach

you that later. Just start 'em down my tracks and they'll follow."

"How do I stop them?"

"You beller WHOA!" He dug into his pocket and grasped a handful of brown, lumpy sugar. "And at the end of each day, after they been unhitched and watered and fed, you pat 'em on the neck and work their ears gentle, and put a little piece of this in the flat of your hand and let 'em eat it. That tells 'em they done good. Shove this in yer pocket for now. I'll get more later when it's gone."

Stump wrinkled his forehead in deep thought as he studied Trace for a minute, his doubts showing on his face. He bobbed his head. "Okay. That gets us started for today. I'll help you harness each mornin' like I done today until you get the hang of it. First water stop is two hours out. Let's get crackin'."

He strode off purposefully to the lead wagon.

Trace called after him, "Which wagon am I supposed to drive?"

Stump grasped his whip handle and turned back. "I got the lead. You got the middle. Gimp is last. Just watch me when I start, and wait a minute, and then do what I did. And do it right!"

"What happens if I tip the wagon over? How much do you lose?"

"It won't matter."

"Why?"

"Because stuck in there under all the drygoods is thirty-two cases of dynamite."

Stump immediately turned back and his whip cracked like a rifleshot as he bellered "Pull you lop-eared heathens. Pull. Tulip, Rose, you pull." The whip cracked again, and the huge, broad, seven-foot iron-rimmed wheels of the old freight wagon creaked and began to turn.

At the word *dynamite* Trace went numb. He slumped to his knees for an instant in stark, unbridled horror. His eyes went glassy and the pupils drew to a pinpoint. Then he leaped to his feet with an agility never before known by him, and he bellowed "Dynamite?"

Stump turned back and his face was the picture of surprise, followed by wrath. He bellered back, "Trace, get them mules moving. Now."

Trace licked suddenly dry lips and backed away from the wagon. A pistol-shot whip crack not far behind brought him up short and he turned to see Stump trotting towards him. Again the whip cracked, and Trace saw the rage in Stump's face. The vision of Stretch and Pot and Harley sprawled out on the back room floor of the saloon flicked through his brain, and in two giant steps he reached his whip. He raised it high and laid it out behind him, and then snapped it forward. It cracked like spring river ice.

"Pull you lop-eared heathens. Buttercup, you there Daisy, you pull or I'll skin you alive. Bess, Belle, you dig in you slab-sided coyote baits. Zeb, Zeke, pull or we have mule stew for supper!"

So loud did he beller that horses and mules in town paced nervously, and lights flickered on in some of the houses. A few people walked out barefoot, wearing only long-handled underwear, to stare. Harley and Pot and Stretch stood in the gray dawn of the dusty street in amazement. Stretch muttered, "Danged if that new dude ain't a muleskinner after all."

45

At the second crack from Trace's whip, twelve long ears snapped erect, and twenty-four hooves dug in. For the first ten feet they dug craters where they strained and sunk in, and then the wagon was rolling and the mules settled into their pulling stride.

Trace looked at the cracking, moving, rumbling monster, face white as a bedsheet. As though the words were coming from the lips of someone else, he barked "Buttercup, you keep your feet out of those trace chains." The whip cracked. He bellered "Zeb, you quit laying back and pull." The whip cracked.

Stump's jaw went slack and he stood for a moment in disbelief before he spun and ran back to his own wagon.

Two hours later Stump stopped his team at the first water hole and turned, holding his breath to see if Trace could stop the heavy wagon.

"Whoa you lop-eared scoundrels, whoa or I'll skin you alive." The whip cracked and the wagon stopped. Trace backed up a step and wilted into a heap, sitting in the dirt, as the whip fell from his hands. Stump walked quickly to his side.

"Trace, you done real good. Real good."

"Dynamite!" Trace's chin dropped and he could only stare at the ground. "You could have killed us all." He hacked a cough.

"Well," Stump said in his raspy voice as he raised his generous jowl and scratched the scraggly whisker growth, "That mighta been a little risky maybe, but considerin' what it done towards makin' you a first-class muleskinner, well, it all worked out just fine."

"Thirty-two cases of dynamite," was all Trace mumbled, sitting in the dirt, staring at the ground.

Through the day, Trace bellowed orders in Mule and his whip cracked like a pistol as he walked beside them, guiding them around rocks or holes that would jostle the deadly cargo. Pain stabbed as stiff boots raised blisters on tender feet, then broke them, bleeding. The leather-wrapped stock of the whip curled his palms and fingers, then blistered them and broke the blisters. Trace said nothing, but held his place in the column and marched doggedly on, head tipped back to stare through his glasses at the tailgate of Stump's wagon.

The sun turned to a great orange ball as it came to rest on the western mountain rim, turning the pristine, unsullied wilderness ablaze with gold and red. Stump finally bellowed his team to a stop by a small spring surrounded by cattails and a few pines. They unhitched, watered, fed, and picketed the mules for the night.

Taking his first assignment as camp cook, Trace wordlessly prepared the supper. Seated around the small, flickering cook fire in gathering dusk, they silently wolfed down gravy, biscuits, beans baked with brown sugar and a touch of vinegar and chopped onions, and a half dozen cinnamon-sugared rolls made from the last of the biscuit dough.

"Trace," Stump said in the silence, "you're plumb full of surprises. This is maybe the best meal I ever et on the trail. Wouldn't you say, Gimp?"

Gimp nodded his approval while he ran his last piece of biscuit around his tin plate to catch all the juice.

"Where'd you learn to cook like that?"

Trace ached everywhere. His feet were on fire and he would never use his hands again. He did not turn to look at Stump, but just murmured, "I been doing my own cooking for ten years," and coughed once.

"Well, you sure learned good." Stump rubbed his belly with both hands for a mintue, feeling pain for what Trace was going through.

"Here, take off your boots," he said, a sudden note of tenderness in his usually gruff voice. "And your socks, and then let me see the palms of your hands." Stump's nose wrinkled as he gently held the feet, then the hands, and carefully went over the bloody, broken blisters and enflamed flesh. "Them is bad. Why didn't you say somethin'?"

"Thirty-two cases of dynamite."

Stump heated water and washed the feet and hands while Trace sucked air through gritted teeth. Then Stump went to his own wagon and rummaged for a minute. "Here" he said, and carefully rubbed a thick, heavy carbolic salve into them. He loosely wrapped them in clean strips of sheeting from his own war bag.

"Leave 'em wrapped like that 'til mornin' and we'll do it again and bind 'em good. Wear two pair of socks tomorrow. I got some old winter gloves you can use. That'll help."

After they crawled into their blankets under a jet-black crystal sky pierced with a hundred million points of light, Stump quietly said in the darkness, "Trace, you done real good today."

Slowly, in barely audible, whispered tones, Stump heard, "Thirty-two cases of dynamite!" There was a tiny cough, and then only the deep breathing of bone-weary, exhausted sleep.

5

"Lose somethin'?" Stump looked at Trace, face pinched in question. Trace was on his hands and knees, carefully patting the dust near Belle's feet.

"I was hitching up Belle when my glasses fell off. I can't find them."

Placing his feet carefully, Stump walked to Trace's side and bent low, searching. "Here they are." He reached inside the trace chain, near Belle's hind feet, and picked the glasses from the dirt, then shook his head sadly. "But it looks like Belle stepped on 'em. They are sure enough busted."

Trace stood, and Stump put the twisted wreckage in his hand. Trace felt them for a moment, then slowly shook his head. "I can't see without them." He raised them close to his face to peer at them, bewildered.

"Think you can handle your team?" Stump asked hesitantly.

"I can't see them. Only dim shapes."

Stump took off his hat and scratched his head. "Well if that don't beat all. It's twelve days back for another muleskinner, or four days to the Settlement. And there sure ain't no spare muleskinners at the Settlement. Or we can leave the wagon here and come back for what's left of it after the thieves get finished. Goldang the cussed goldang luck." He stomped impatiently a few steps and jammed his hands on his hips.

Trace slowly slipped the ruined glasses into his shirt pocket and turned towards his team, head bowed. Suddenly, from nowhere, an unfamiliar, nearly frightening feeling crept into his breast. Stump had depended on him, and now Stump needed him badly. For the first time in his life, what he did made a difference to someone. He swallowed hard as strange new feelings swelled throughout his entire being. This was his team! He was responsible!

He stood in shock as he realized his own next thoughts. I can do this! I can hitch up this team and I can drive this wagon to the Settlement. I can do it! I will do it! He swallowed again as a voice inside shouted, "You're crazy!" He set his jaw and exhaled a great breath. "Yes, I'm crazy, but I can do it, and I *will!*"

Hesitantly, he reached a trembling hand until it bumped the rump of a mule. "Belle," he said softly, and felt the muscles tighten and knew she had turned her head to him as usual when he spoke to her while hitching her up. "Good girl. Stand easy. Just hitching you up." He patted her, and she settled down, waiting patiently.

His hands reached for the trace chain, and he felt for the ring on the singletree. He snapped the hook into place and walked forward, feeling for the horse collar for Buttercup. Steadily, methodically, he felt his way through the hitch-up of the team, then patted his way down the side of the wagon until he found his whip.

"Stump, you there?" he turned and called.

"Right here. And I can't believe what you just done."

"Let's give it a try. If I get in trouble I'll stop. Just look back once in a while. You too, Gimp, keep an eye forward." He paused. "What if I hit a rock or a hole?"

Hope resounding in his voice, Stump answered, "I pass 'em before you do. If any of 'em looks bad I'll sing out. You sure about this? I mean, you ain't forgot about what you're carrying in that wagon?"

"Not for one second. Let's roll 'em."

The whips cracked, and the men bellowed. The mules obediently leaned into their harnesses and the wagons groaned forward. Trace set his jaw and watched. When the dark blur of the massive wagon moved, he walked with it. He discovered that he could keep pace by tapping the wagon side with the whip from time to time. Twice before noon and once after the noon meal, he stumbled over rocks or roots, but bounded back to his feet and kept his wagon moving with the others. When they stopped to make evening camp, Trace unhitched his team by feel and followed Stump and Gimp to the stream where they watered the animals, then fed them and hobbled them for the night. Trace pulled the magic brown sugar from his pocket and patted each one on the neck. "You did good," he repeated to them in a low voice while he palmed the lumps and they reached to gratefully take them.

He took his turn at cooking supper, and only once did he gasp when he accidentally touched the side of the skillet, rather than the handle.

"Burned?" Stump inquired. "Want me to finish?"

Trace shook his head. "I'm all right. It won't happen again."

Stump raised his chin and scratched his throat as he watched Trace finish. "Pecky beggar," he murmured to himself admiringly. "Dang pecky."

While they worked on the last of the biscuits, covered generously with sweet molasses, Stump said, "I never asked you because it ain't right to pry into another man's business. But just what is it got you so all fired determined to get to the Settlement?"

Gimp paused and looked up, waiting.

"The President of the United States."

Stump froze and his chin dropped nearly to his belly button. Gimp dropped half a biscuit in the dirt.

"Insane!" Stump exclaimed, eyes popping out of his head. "The dynamite has drove you insane!"

I am under orders to make an investigation of an Indian uprising that destroyed a lot of medicinal alcohol a few weeks ago."

Stump choked on a biscuit. "A what?"

"Uprising. The Blackfeet Indians."

Gimp fell off his log and laid in the dirt in a laughing fit.

"You talkin' about Lump and Injun Charlie and them two others that tried to snitch a barrel of old Lumley's moonshine and accidentally blew two barges to smithereens?"

"That isn't what I was told. The Blackfoot nation attacked in the middle of the night and set fire to medical supplies intended for the local citizens. Plundering. Fire. Explosions. Attacks. A total, bloody rebellion."

52

Minutes passed while Stump joined Gimp on the ground, unable to control paroxysms of laughter. Wheezing, face beet red, he finally rallied enough to raise onto one elbow and asked, "Who told you that story?"

"Benjamin Harrison, President of the United States. I have his signed letter of authority in my coat pocket to come here, see the rebellion firsthand, take whatever emergency steps are necessary, and report back to him."

Stump collapsed again, begging for mercy as he began to wheeze from the hysteria seizure. Gimp was whimpering through his laughter, from the pain in his aching sides.

Trace sat on his log munching the last of his biscuits and molasses, while he strained to see the blurred shapes writhing on the ground. The wheezing and laughter finally subsided, and Stump raised to a sitting position while Gimp just laid flat on his back, too weak to move.

"You got a few problems," Stump finally said. "In the memory of anyone in this part of the country, no Blackfoot ever got into a rebellion. They're plumb peaceful. Right now, the most beloved four men for a thousand miles any direction are Lump, Injun Charlie, Drinks Much, and Mole. They're the ones that blew the barges."

Again Stump flopped over in a laughing fit, and Gimp, flat on his back, just stared at the sky and whined in pain.

Trace scratched his head and waited until Stump again came under control. "Most beloved?"

"Sure. Nobody ever saw a fireworks treat like

the one those four put on, whatwith the river on fire and kegs blowin' up all over the place, some hundreds of feet in the air. Folks clean over at Fort Lemhi got out of bed in the middle of the night to watch. And then, eight or nine hundred barrels got loose in the river and you never seen the river so jammed with boats and anything that would float, from the Settlement clean to the Pacific Ocean. The soldier boys at Fort Lemhi fetched nine, fifty-gallon barrels out of the river, waited about twenty minutes for the owner to make claim, then disposed of it. The disposin' took 'em about two days workin' around the clock, and they spent the next fifteen days recoverin'. Six of 'em still can't see good. That was two weeks of the dangdest whingding this territory ever saw. I reckon Lump could beat Ben Harrison for President out here if the election was held right now."

Trace set his empty plate in the dirt and murmured quietly, "Moonshine? That wasn't medicinal alcohol?"

"Land-a-mercy, they was more than sixteen thousand gallons of it. Sixteen thousand gallons of medicinal alcohol would have treated every man, woman, child, horse, mule, and jackass within a thousand miles for anything that ailed them for twenty years! That was pure moonshine!"

Trace interlaced his fingers in deep thought. "Where did it come from?"

"If I was you, I'd be askin' Gideon Lumley that question."

"Who's Gideon Lumley?"

"Lives on the Montana side of the Snake River,

right across from the Settlement. Stories has it he owned that moonshine, and was so cussed mad when it got blowed up that he wrote the President."

"What did he plan to do with sixteen thousand gallons of moonshine whiskey?"

"You'll have to ask him. One thing sure. He didn't intend disinfecting no wounds sustained by the pilgrims out here." Stump's mouth watered at the thought of sixteen thousand gallons of moonshine, and he wiped it on his sleeve.

Trace slowly nodded and reached to the ground, feeling for his tin plate and cup to wash them before he laid out his bedroll for the night. "Guess I'll just ask Mr. Lumley."

6

Kate felt the ground vibrations through the floor before she heard the sounds, and closed her eyes to concentrate on the soles of her feet. Quickly she wiped her hands on her apron and tossed it aside as she hurried out into the heat of the July sun at the back of the old, ramshackle Cataldo Mission. She shaded her eyes with one hand as she trotted towards the far edge of the clearing, one hundred yards distant, eyes searching. Through the lodgepole pines she saw them coming. Three huge freight wagons, eighteen mules, and three men.

She broke into a trot, waving while her moccasins raised small curls of dust. Her woolen men's pants, rolled halfway to her knees, were held up by a single suspender, and the old, blue cotton shirttail was stuffed inside the waistband, giving her a billowy look as she hurried along.

"Kate! Bless you for a sight straight from heaven," Stump shouted. "Pull, you there, Tulip and Rose."

Kate waited until they reached her, then fell in beside Stump and slipped her arm through his. They continued back to the shady side of the old, huge building, where Stump stopped his wagon and waited for Trace and Gimp to stop theirs. Then he turned and bear hugged Kate off the ground while she hugged him back. Stump swung Kate in one complete turnaround with her long, deep auburn hair tied back by a piece of rawhide flying behind her. He set her back on the ground, and her green eyes flashed as a huge grin spread.

"Kate Darlin', every time I see you I know why I keep comin' back here with freight. How are you. How you been?"

"Fit as a fiddle and doin' fine. But I missed you, you old badger. Only difference between you and one of them mules is they got a little longer ears, but I sure have missed you anyway. How you been?"

"Havin' so much fun it's sinful," he said, grinning. "Business holdin'? You sure you can use all these goods?"

"Most of them are already sold. By fall they'll all be picked up and we can talk about another load before winter sets in. Come on in where it's cool and have a drink of cold apple cider. Got the jug sunk in the well."

"You go fetch it while me and the boys tend the teams. Then we'll be in and get caught up on everything."

Half an hour later the three men blinked as they passed from the bright sunlight into the big, cool room at the back of the old, abandoned mission, where Kate ran her general trading post. Everything needed for life on the frontier, from smoked meat to axe handles, was arranged in a sort of comfortable muddle, with all the rich, pungent smells reaching out to tantalize.

Kate plunked four tin cups onto a plank table in

the middle of the room, and pulled a corncob from the neck of an old crock jug. She carefully poured all the cups full and Stump and Gimp raised theirs as Kate spoke. "Here's to the guardian angel that got you and your wagons here safe again."

Stump answered, "Here's to you, Kate, the guardian angel."

Kate blushed at Stump's unabashed flattery while Stump guided Trace's probing hand to his cup, and they all took their first taste of the sweet, cool cider, then sat down at the table.

A shadow passed over Kate's face as she studied Trace and realized he was nearly blind. She looked meaningfully at Stump, who took his cue from her.

"Oh, Kate, this here is Trace. Buckshot run off again with that dark-haired vixen and I had to hire a new muleskinner. This here is him. Belle stepped on his eyeglasses a few days ago and he's just learnin' to get along without 'em. Trace, this here is Kate."

Kate reached her hand across the table, man fashion, to shake hands, but Trace could only see a dark blur make a small move, and didn't know her hand was extended. Kate took his hand in hers and shook it.

"Sorry, Miss Kate. My pleasure meeting you," Trace said.

"I'm happy to meet you, Trace," she said, and shook her head slightly. How could a man with such poor vision survive in the wilderness? "Sorry about the eyeglasses," she continued, and for a moment she studied him, making the usual frontier appraisal of a stranger.

"Trace is here on official business," Stump said.

"Sent here by the President of these here Yewnited States to look into the moonshine bonfire we had a little while back."

Kate's eyes widened. "Any special reason?"

Stump looked at Trace and waited for the answer.

"No," Trace said, "he just wanted to be sure we didn't have a full scale Blackfoot uprising out here."

Kate threw back her head and her rich laugh echoed off the walls. Trace turned his eyes towards her, then back to Stump. In his entire life in the high society of Baltimore and Washington, D.C., he had never heard a woman throw back her head and laugh like she really meant it. A tiny smile passed over his face, and a strange look flickered in his eyes for a moment.

"Blackfoot *what?*" Kate asked.

"Uprising," Trace said, and smiled and shook his head expectantly. Again Kate laughed, and Trace glanced at Stump and shrugged.

"The uprising consisted of four shy Blackfoot Indians who accidentally gave us the best show and celebration we've had around here as far back as memory goes."

"So Stump said," Trace said quietly. "It involved about sixteen thousand gallons of moonshine. How do I find a man named Gideon Lumley?"

"You're on the right track," said Kate. "Just across the Snake River. There's a boat dock at the Elijah Hubbard place on this side. I'll show you, soon as we get some of those drygoods unloaded. I can't wait to see the laces and dresses and frilly things. We got some women around here been waiting for months."

The chatter mellowed and continued for a while before Stump said, "Reckon we better unload the goods from Trace's wagon and get that dynamite away from the building. Hate to have a storm come up and lightning set it off."

They all rose and walked back outside to begin the labor of unloading the wagon. While they worked, Trace quietly studied the old, battered, bullet- and cannon-pocked building with the iron battle shutters that could be closed against shot and arrows. He watched as occasionally the dim shapes of bearded mountain men dressed in aging leather, and Chinese railroad laborers in pants that wrapped around, and Indians with braids and flinty eyes, came and went.

The shadows grew longer as the sun settled towards the western mountain rim. By dusk they had unloaded boxed dresses, laces, bolts of colored cloth, canned goods, two dozen rifles, sixty sides of bacon, ten cases of hams, and two cases of Bibles. All that remained in Trace's wagon was thirty-two cases of dynamite, tied down securely. The three men carefully rolled the giant wagon a hundred yards down the slight eastern incline, into the timber, and chocked the wheels. As they walked back to the mission, shoulder to shoulder, Kate walked from the building.

"Come and get it while it's warm."

They sat down at a table crowded with steaming bowls and rich smells and Stump said, "It's sinful to talk while you're eatin' Kate's cookin'."

And so it was. Kate called for silence and bowed her head. "Father, we're thankful to be together as friends and loved ones at this table. Bless these victuals, and bless us with good sense to use the strength from them in doing good things. Amen."

Never had food tasted better. Platters and bowls of mashed potatoes drenched with gravy, peas, and carrots were passed until they were empty, followed by mountain blueberries with sugar and thick cream, cold cider, and one quarter of a deep-dish mince pie. The men chewed and swallowed slowly, in near total silence, eyes often closed as they gloried in the eating. Finally, Stump wiped his mouth and turned to Kate in reverence. "There ain't no words I know to say how good that was. So I won't try. But if I was thirty years younger I would go get me a bath and shave this ugly kisser of mine, and beg you to marry me."

Kate ducked her head and grinned her embarrassment. "I'll marry you now, if you'll ask."

"I'm too old and sot in my ways, and besides, you wouldn't do it anyway," he replied, and their laughter rang from the walls.

With the supper dishes cleared away, Kate turned to Trace. "We still have enough daylight to get to the river and back, if you would like to see Hubbard's boat dock and let me point out the Lumley place across the river."

Half an hour later she stopped on a rise overlooking the broad ribbon of the Snake River, glowing golden in the sunset behind them. "There's Elijah Hubbard's home," she said, pointing to her right, up a little incline, into the emerald-green pines. She pointed down the slope. "Down there's his boat dock."

Trace squinted. The home was a blur. The boat dock was a light-colored splotch joining the broad, green-brown river.

"Over there, straight across the river, is the Lumley land. His boat dock is there. His house is three, four miles inland, a little north of due east from the dock. You will likely find him home tomorrow."

Trace nodded. "Thanks. I think I will pay him a visit. But before I do, I would like to talk with Mr. Lump. How could I find him?"

"Word's out about Stump's wagons getting here, and it's a big day around here when the freight arrives. By dawn tomorrow, Lump and most everybody within twenty miles will be here. Stump uses Lump and Injun Charlie and Drinks Much and Mole to help unload the wagons, and load the furs for the return trip. They eat and sleep right here until he pulls out."

They matched stride for stride walking back to the trading post. Trace asked, "Is there a ferry across the river?"

"Eight miles upstream. We row across from here."

"Can I rent a boat?"

"Use mine. My name's on the front."

"Thanks. Where were the barges tied when they blew up?"

"Quarter of a mile below Hubbard's boat dock, on the edge of Hubbard's land. They were hidden by brush and cattails."

Dusk deepened as they returned to the trading post. Stump had already lighted the lamps inside, and the place was a cheery jumble of stacked goods bathed in yellow lantern glow.

"You're back," Stump said from the table, where he and Gimp were working on the cider jug.

"Yes," Trace said. "How long before you make the return trip to Pocatello?"

"A little over a week. We got to rest the mules a little while we load up the furs from last winter. Kate stores 'em upstairs. Injun Charlie and his three friends are hired to help."

Trace nodded his head and sat down at the table. "Miss Kate, thanks for your help at the river."

"My pleasure." She began sorting out the ladies dresses and garments.

Talk and chatter and chiding and laughter went on for an hour before the men took their leave, and all bedded down beneath the wagons by the trading post.

"Trace," said Kate, laughing, "meet this real dangerous Indian named Lump."

In the gray light of early dawn, Trace turned from the well where he was drawing water to wash, towards the sound of Kate's voice, and squinted at the five indistinct shapes moving towards him. He thrust out his hand towards the one resembling a freight wagon and waited. He felt a monstrous hand enclose his own, and sucked a quick breath as his hand went numb.

"Pleased to make your acquaintance, Mr. Lump," he said through gritted teeth.

Lump gave Trace's hand one mighty pump and released it, grinning from ear to ear at the absurd novelty of the white man's strange custom of squeezing hands.

"White man speak with forked tongue," he said, glowing with pride in his ability to remember and repeat the white man's words.

Trace glanced at Kate and she explained, "That's all the English he knows and he uses it every chance he gets. Hasn't got a hint of what it means."

"Is he normal?" Trace whispered, then looked nearly straight up at the huge, round blur of the grinning face."

"What's normal?" Kate responded. "His body got huge but his mind quit growing when he was about five. He loves everyone. Never intentionally hurt a soul that didn't have it coming. Once he likes you, he's your friend forever. I wish everybody was as normal as Lump."

Trace considered for a moment, then dug a chunk of Stump's brown mule sugar from his pocket and extended it towards Lump. Hesitantly Lump plucked it from his palm and plopped it into his mouth. Instantly his eyes closed as he savored the thick sweetness.

Kate looked at Trace. "I think you just made a friend forever. Now shake hands with Injun Charlie, Drinks Much, and Mole, and we'll all go inside for some flapjacks and coffee. This crew has to get busy.

The men shook hands with nods and greetings, then followed Kate back inside the old mission where the table was set, waiting. They settled onto chairs while Kate brought two platters of golden-brown, smoking pancakes, and a gallon-sized, blue enamelled coffee pot. The rich aroma reached inside the men, who seized their knives and forks.

"Hold on there," Kate ordered with a chuckle. "You gents bow your heads while we return thanks for these good things."

Injun Charlie whispered to Lump, who instantly dropped his fork, folded his great arms, and bowed his head like a child. The other men silently bowed their heads.

"Father, we're thankful for the bounties of this good earth," Kate said, "and we're thankful to be here together as friends and loved ones. Bless this food and bless us to use it right. Amen."

Forks speared smoking pancakes, and the homemade butter plate made the rounds, followed by the steaming coffee pot.

"Please pass the syrup," Trace said, and turned towards Kate. "Once I'm on the Montana side of the river, is there a road to Lumley's place?" He drenched four huge buttery pancakes with syrup.

"A wagon trail. But with your glasses broke I don't think you better try it alone. I talked with Injun Charlie and he'll go with you. He knows the most English and how to find the Lumley place."

"What about the others?"

"We'd need a barge for Lump. They'll stay here."

"Pass the coffee. Is Lumley apt to be any trouble?"

Stump sucked noisily at his steaming coffee mug and cut into the conversation. "Old Lumley is slippery, and in a showdown he might get mean. If he gets ornery you back outta there and come tell us."

Trace smiled at the remembrance of Stump and the pick handle getting his clothes back in the back room of the Pocatello saloon. "I'll do that. Kate, those were the best pancakes I ever had. I better get across the river. Is Injun Charlie ready?"

Injun Charlie stuffed the last of his pancakes in his mouth and stood, ready.

"Stump, keep track of the time I'm gone with part of your crew. I'll get a government voucher so you can get your money back."

"You got a deal."

At the edge of the clearing Trace paused to wave back at the fuzzy images, and then fell in behind Injun Charlie, who set a pace through the straight, clean pines, their tops glowing in the shine of the rising sun. Trace yearned to see the resplendently glorious morning as he breathed the tangy scent of the forest.

At the river's edge, Injun Charlie steered him to Kate's boat and got him seated, then cast off the rope and shoved the boat adrift before he settled onto the seat beside Trace. "You pull oar, I pull oar," he said.

Trace nodded and grasped his oar, feeling until he knew he had the handle. He began to pull.

"No!" exclaimed Injun Charlie. "You pull when I pull." He grasped the side of the boat while his head stopped spinning from the two circles the boat had made when Trace pulled.

"Okay." Trace watched and stroked when Injun Charlie did. Twenty minutes later Trace felt the bow of the boat bump solid, and Injun Charlie quickly shipped his oar and scrambled up to tie the boat to the Lumley dock. "Come careful," he said, waiting while Trace walked forward, then stepped onto the dock.

"Lumley place there." Injun Charlie pointed due east and settled into a steady pace, Trace following closely. Forty minutes later they crested a small rise in the sagebrush and Injun Charlie stopped, waiting for Trace. "Lumley place just over rise."

Trace wrinkled his nose at the acrid bite of a ghastly, putrid odor. "What's that horrible smell?" He peered ahead, seeing nothing but the hazy outline of the top of the rise. He waited, certain Injun Charlie, a true son of the wilderness, would know.

Charlie sniffed and wrinkled his nose. "Don't smell nothing."

"You can't smell that?" Trace asked in disbelief.

"No smell nothing." Injun Charlie turned and again resumed the pace.

At the top of the rise the odor nearly knocked Trace to his knees. Injun Charlie paused and thrust his huge hawk nose into the air and sniffed three times loudly. His eyes narrowed and he looked wise.

"Slight odor near Lumley place," he muttered, and continued his march.

Trace held his breath until he saw spots, then gasped for air that was more nauseating than the last. With a quarter mile yet to go, the rank, acrid odor was making Trace lightheaded. "Injun Charlie, I can't take much more of this. What's causing it?"

"Don't know. Over there."

"Take me."

Minutes later Injun Charlie slowed in a clearing three hundred yards south of the Lumley house. Before him was a horrendous pile of oozing brown stuff held within a solid fence of pine boards, two feet high. The entire enclosure was surrounded by pigs and mules, all making strange sounds that melded into an unbelievable, unearthly din, and none of them were moving.

Trace walked past Injun Charlie, face thrust forward, squinting, trying to make the hazy shapes take solid form in the unearthly uproar. His foot struck an inert body and a grunt startled him. He thrust his face down, and there, three inches off the end of his nose, was a pig laying flat on its back, all four legs in the air. It stared straight back up at him, making whining sounds never before heard in the genus swine. The pig's breath all but knocked Trace unconscious.

Trace jerked straight in shock. "Pigs," he blurted in the torrent of whines and groans and grunts and brays.

"Maybe three hundred pigs, one hundred mules," Injun Charlie said.

"What?" Trace gasped. He leaned and strained to see, but could only make out the inert shapes while the sounds continued.

"What's that pile of stuff?" he gasped, gesturing, trying to hold his breath.

"Don't know."

"What are all these animals doing?"

"Nothing. Lay down, fall down, sit down. No move."

"They aren't moving?"

"No move. Stay still, whine, make strange noise."

"Cholera? Are they dying?"

"No. Look drunk."

"Drunk!" Trace jerked straight in disbelief. He thrust out his hands and began feeling his way among the disoriented animals. He brushed a mule and felt his way to the head. The mule was sitting on its hindquarters, its nose pointed straight at the sun-drenched sky, long ears hung back while it uttered a sort of whimpering, pleading, braying sound, totally unaware Trace was even there. Trace continued walking, struck dumb as he felt more mules and pigs in every posture known in the animal kingdom, simply whining and whimpering.

"Men come," said Injun Charlie, pointing west. "Look mean. We go to Lumley house."

Trace heard the slight strain in Injun Charlie's voice and walked towards him, noticing for the first time that six dim shapes were approaching from the trees behind the clearing. Hastily he followed Injun Charlie towards the house.

A booming shout brought their heads around. "Hey, you, hold on there or we shoot."

Injun Charlie stopped, and Trace bumped into him before he could stop, and they stood still, waiting. "Shouldn't we shout something back," Trace whispered out of the side of his mouth as the men approached. "Maybe something like 'drop those guns or we'll go on the war path'?"

"You shout about war path," Injun Charlie said instantly. "I surrender." Injun Charlie did not change his expression as the six men hastened up.

The leader, a burly, surly man with a square jaw covered with a week's growth of dark beard stubble confronted them with a huge Navy Colt revolver clutched in his hand. "What you doing here on private land?"

Injun Charlie eyed the man behind him, who had a bald head that shone in the morning sunlight. The man's eyebrows were burned very short.

Trace stared at the fuzzy shapes before him. "My name is Dinwoody and . . ."

The instant cackle of raucous laughter from all six men cut him off and rang in the pines a quarter mile distant.

The leader gasped for air and held his laughter long enough to blurt "Your name is *what?*"

"Dinwoody, and I . . ."

The six men exploded again, grasping their sides in a paroxysm of laughter.

Injun Charlie raised both eyebrows at once, for the first time in his life, and turned to Trace. "What happened to Trace?"

Trace looked at Injun Charlie, irritated, and continued.

"My name is Dinwoody and I have been sent here by the U.S. government to investigate a claim by Gideon Lumley that he lost a fortune when Indians raided his store of medicinal alcohol. I understand Mr. Lumley lives here."

The men sniggered at the words "medicinal alcohol," and their leader replied, "Well now, how do we know you're from the government?"

"I have a letter here from the president of the United States." Trace pulled it from inside his shirt.

The bearded man scowled. "Let me see it," he barked, and raised his pistol.

Trace handed it to him. He raised it to eye level, upside down, and pretended to read for several seconds. "Looks real," he said importantly, and thrust it back to Trace. Follow us. We work for Lumley and he will sure want to talk to you."

Five minutes later Trace was standing on the porch of the old, run-down Lumley cabin while Gideon Lumley hitched his last suspender over his shoulder and opened the plank door that leaned on leather hinges. "You from the government?" he asked suspiciously while the door banged behind him. "Can you prove it?"

Trace handed him the letter. Lumley stepped off

the porch and turned to catch the sunlight, then read, his lips silently and slowly making out each word. He frowned, "If you're here to get my money back from them thievin' murderin' redskins, why you got one of them with you? He's just as guilty as them other Blackfoot heathens who done it."

Startled, Trace fumbled for something to say.

Injun Charlie took one firm step forward. "Me not Blackfoot," he said. "Me Apache. Hate Blackfeet. Take many Blackfeet scalp. Help get money back from Blackfeet."

Trace turned a stunned expression towards Injun Charlie and whispered. "Are you nuts? What are you doing?"

An instant look of disbelief seized Lumley. "You're an Apache? You don't look like no Apache. What you doing up here in these parts?"

"Come with Geronimo. Go to Canada, start uprising." Injun Charlie folded his arms and looked fierce.

"Ha! Last I heard Geronimo gave up and went onto the reservation down in New Mexico or somewhere," Lumley said triumphantly. Then his forehead wrinkled as he struggled to remember what he had heard, and when, and from whom.

"That his brother go to reservation. Geronimo no go on reservation. Plenty bad Apache. Come north. Bring many warrior with him. We go take Canada."

Lumley snorted. "All right, if you're Apache, what's your name?"

Injun Charlie slowly lowered his arms. His upper lip curled in contempt while he froze Lumley in his tracks with a horrible expression in both his eagle eyes. "Me Cochise. White man ask one more dumb question, Cochise come back tomorrow with Geronimo warriors. We wipe all pigs, mules from earth. Take Lumley, all men prisoner. Apaches have one hundred eighty-two ancient tortures, sixty-nine new ones. Use them all on Lumley and his men. Take five days, maybe six. Then we take all scalps except for man over there with skin for hair, and head like cannonball. He have no hair, so we take whole head. Then we burn place to ground."

Injun Charlie took a menacing step forward, and Lumley recoiled, his face ashen gray. He raised an arm defensively. "Now hold on there, Cochise. Ain't no call to get peeved about this. Mr. Dinwoody only wants some information." He turned to Trace, nearly pleading. "Now what was it you wanted to know, Mr. Dinwoody?" The color began to return to his face.

Trace looked at Injun Charlie as though he had never met him before, then turned to Lumley. "Do you have any records of how much medicinal alcohol was seized by the Indians?"

"Sixteen thousand gallons."

"How long did it take to prepare it?"

"Over a year. Maybe fifteen months."

"Was it under contract for sale to the pioneers and settlers?"

"Why sure, absolutely. We had orders for it all up and down the Snake River. We stored it in barges to make deliveries."

"What price?"

"One dollar a gallon. A bargain. Ninety cents for fifty gallons or more."

"About $16,000 worth," Trace continued.

"Yes."

"If I write that up the way you told it, would you sign it so I can submit it with my report and request for your money?"

"Dang tootin.' "

"What's all that stuff down there inside the fence where the pigs and mules are?"

"That is a brand new idee for feeding livestock. Goin' to sell hams and bacon and sausage, and pack mules to the settlers that are starting to come."

"But what is that pile of brown stuff they're eating?"

"Well, uh, well . . ." Lumley fumbled for a moment before he blurted, "That's a new secret formula mush that we invented for livestock feed. Fattens 'em up real fast and it's cheap. We're goin' to get a genuine patent on it when we finish testin' 'er out."

Trace looked at Injun Charlie for a moment, then said to Lumley, "I will make up a written report and see you again in the next couple of days to get it signed. I have just a few more things I must do to finish my investigation." Trace started to go.

Injun Charlie suddenly strode to the man with the big Navy Colt revolver shoved into his belt. He seized the pistol and threw it into the dirt at his feet. He stood toe to toe, nose to nose with the man for two or three seconds, eyes glistening like flecks of obsidian.

"You pick up pistol before Cochise out of sight, you wake up tomorrow morning with big question about missing scalp."

The man swallowed hard and tried to cover his

panic by nodding violently and smiling his whole-hearted understanding.

Injun Charlie turned back to Trace. "We go now. White men harmless. No fight. No nothing. Just raise pigs, mules." He marched contemptuously away, Trace following close behind. Injun Charlie did not look back until they had passed the crest of the hill and Lumley and his men were out of sight.

Trace blurted, "You *crazy?* Cochise! He died back in '74. And what was the idea with that pistol and those threats? You lost your mind?"

"No lose mind. Save our lives. Trace do nothing when man pull gun, so Injun Charlie have to fix." Charlie glanced nervously over his shoulder. "We move a little faster." He broke into a ground-eating trot, with the peculiar, slight side-to-side rocking motion of a man who has covered long distances many times before.

"They'll kill us when they find out you lied," Trace exclaimed as he labored to keep up with Injun Charlie. "Where did you learn to lie and put on an act like that?"

"Study white man for thirty years. Learn real good about lie, act mean."

" They're comin'," Stump bellowed as he ran a sleeve across his sweaty face. He turned from the stack of freight he had been sorting to watch the two men emerge from the timber at the edge of the clearing. Kate walked out of the trading post and together they hurried to meet Injun Charlie and Trace.

"Well, what happened?" Kate called to them.

In less than twenty seconds Injun Charlie summed it all up while they walked back to the trading post. Inside, they all sat down and Kate poured cider.

"What did you think of Lumley?" Kate asked as Trace sipped.

Trace squinted at her fuzzy image. "I don't know yet. There are a lot of things he didn't tell me. I wish I knew what that pile of smelly stuff was and what it was doing to those pigs and mules. Why does he have six tough guys guarding the place?" He shook his head dubiously. "Something's wrong over there."

"Skin-headed man on barge when fire start," Injun Charlie volunteered. "Lump thump him."

"Well," Stump said decisively, "If you want to know what that pile of stuff is, let's send Mole. He's the best sneaker this side of the Mississippi."

Mole brightened and smiled from ear to ear. "Mole find out."

76

After supper, when full darkness had settled, Mole beamed in purest delight. "Be back by morning," was all he said, and disappeared into the shadows before they knew he had moved. The others sat around the table gathering gumption to help Kate with the dishes, and bed down under the wagons for the night.

Trace spoke to Stump. "What do you make medicinal alcohol from?"

Stump scratched his beard. "I don't know exactly. Wood I think. But that don't make no diferrence because we're dealin' with moonshine here, and that's made from wheat mash, and it sure has nothin' to do with medicine."

"Regular wheat, like for bread?"

"Yep."

"How much wheat to make sixteen thousand gallons of moonshine?"

"Ain't never made none of that white lightnin' myself, so I don't know. But I reckon it would take a mountain of it."

"Where would Lumley get that much wheat out here?"

"It's a cinch he never grew it," Stump retorted while he stretched and yawned. "The only person within three hundred miles of here that handles that much wheat is old Amos Klungbottom. He runs the gov'ment Indian Agency office that doles out rations to the Indians, eight miles west of here. The agency might handle that much wheat in a year or two."

Stump stopped cold in his tracks and locked eyes with Kate. She jerked around towards Injun Charlie.

"Has Klungbottom given you a wheat ration the past couple of years?"

The room was locked in dead silence as everyone waited on Injun Charlie's response.

"No wheat. Didn't know agency had wheat. Got wormy beans, rotten beef, moldy bacon. No wheat."

Kate faced Trace. "Looks like you better ask Klungbottom a question or two, quick, before Lumley gets to him."

Trace thoughtfully nodded his head while his thoughts ran. "I worked on the accounting records in the Bureau of Indian Affairs in Washignton, D.C. I remember the Klungbottom agency records. You're right. I leave at first light."

"What did them records say about sendin' wheat out here for the Indians?" Stump asked.

"Twelve tons a year," answered Trace. "And if the Indians haven't been getting it, that would be a mountain, in a couple of years."

"We best get some rest," Kate said, "because it looks like life around here's goin' to get interestin' real soon."

They said their good nights and the men walked out to their bedrolls, laid out under the wagons. Ten minutes later the only sounds in the night were nighthawks darting about, and the raucous snoring of Stump.

Kate started at the quiet rap on her door. In the silvery light of a nearly full moon waxing she turned the huge alarm clock and exclaimed, "Two o'clock in the mornin'. Who could that be?" She wrapped her robe tightly and opened the door a foot.

There stood Mole, face split by a huge grin as he

raised an old rusty bucket. The odor hit Kate and she recoiled two steps back into the room and Mole followed her inside and set the bucket on the table. The horrendous stench filled the room instantly and Kate wiped the tears from her eyes as she lighted a lamp.

"What in the name of heaven is that," she demanded of Mole.

"Stuff Lumley feed pigs, mules." His small, hatchet face beamed with pride at his impossible feat of crossing the river, getting a bucketful, and returning, all within five hours, with not one soul the wiser.

"Fetch Stump and the others," Kate directed, and Mole bobbed his head and silently disappeared. Kate followed with the bucket in one hand, her lantern in the other. Moments later the others were gathered to the ring of yellow lamplight cast on the ground.

Trace's nose wrinkled. "That's the smell I was telling you about," he said, holding his breath.

"Mole brought that back from Lumley's. That's what he's feeding those pigs and mules."

Stump's roar of laughter made the mules nervous. "That's sour wheat mash from makin' moonshine! No medicinal alcohol ever come from *that* stuff. It ferments rotten and the stink knocks you out. It's worse than moonshine at makin' you drunk. Most any livestock will eat it, and after about two loads, they can't quit. Why, the bacon and hams from them pigs is probably pickled and cured already and should test out about ninety-six proof. Ought to sell at a premium price, 'specially to them teetotal Mormons." He threw back his head and roared. Bright

79

eyes blinked in the forest as nesting birds and noc-
turnal prowlers blinked and stared and wondered at
the sight of eight clamoring human beings gathered
around a lantern and a bucket.

"Take that thing out in the forest," Kate said to
Mole, "and then come back to my place. I'll get you
some supper and we'll all make a plan. You done
good, Mole."

Mole glowed with pride as he picked up the
bucket and headed into the blackness of the pines.
Injun Charlie followed him twenty yards into the
trees, where they set the bucket inside an old, rotted
log.

Injun Charlie looked back at the clearing for a
moment before he quietly asked, "Any more moonshine at Lumley's?"

"Find maybe ten big barrels, fifty small."

"Bring one back?"

Mole's eyes glistened. "One small keg. Hide
under rock, not far."

Injun Charlie smiled one of his rare smiles and
bobbed his head once. Then they returned to Kate's
place, where they sat at the table with the others.
The talk was serious and low as they worked at making their plan. Finally Trace leaned forward on his
elbows and looked around the table.

"I think that's it. We better get some rest."

The men rose, stretched, said good night to
Kate, and sought their blankets beneath the wagons.
Kate watched from the doorway until they were all
settled in, then closed the door and turned down the
lantern.

Dawn crept across the Settlement clear and

quiet and calm. The men rose to the chatter of the bluejays and the scolding of the squirrels, fed the mules, and washed in icy water on the washstand next to Kate's door. She opened as they finished and announced, "Come get it while it's hot."

Twenty minutes later, patting satisfied stomachs filled with Kate's bacon and eggs and coffee, they walked back into the clear sunlight.

Stump pointed. "The agency's straight that-a-way. Injun Charlie'll get you there."

Two hours later Injun Charlie pointed through the trees at a low, ancient log structure with a sagging roof covered with sod. "Agency there."

Smoke rose from the old, crumbling stone chimney as Trace rapped on the warped plank door.

"Who's there? Come on in," came the rough command from within.

Trace lifted the latch and entered, blinking against the darkness inside, as Injun Charlie silently followed. Trace watched a dim shape rise from behind an old table with one short leg. The man stared at him and then came around the table to face him.

"You ain't no Injun! You here with Injun Charlie? You better state your business, mister, 'cause I ain't givin' no rations to no white man!"

Startled, Trace swallowed and said, "I'm from the U.S. government. I was sent here by President Harrison to investigate the burning of a lot of alcohol, and an Indian rebellion. If you're Amos Klungbottom I need to ask you some questions."

Trace watched the fuzzy image before him move, then stop, sputter and stutter for a moment, then exclaim, "You show up here makin' a claim like that, why that's ridiculous! You don't look like no gov'nment man to me. Who are you?"

Trace handed him the envelope. "Are you Klungbottom?"

"Maybe I am and maybe I ain't."

"If you aren't, give me back that envelope." Trace took a step forward and thrust out his hand. He watched the obscure shape begin to refold the letter, then open it again, glance at the signature once more, refold it, and fumble it into the envelope.

The man fumed, "I never saw the likes of this before. Why, I don't believe . . ."

"Are you Klungbottom or not?" Trace's voice rose.

"Him Klungbottom," Injun Charlie said.

"What right you got comin' here, gettin' into Indian affairs, when you don't know nothin' about them?"

"I'm with the Bureau of Indian Affairs in Washington, D.C. I know all about your agency here. Your account number is I-181. I know about the twenty-four tons of wheat we shipped you, and I know the Indians never saw any of it. So I'll need your books. Now. Get them."

Klungbottom recoiled back against the rickety table and it skittered backwards and threatened to collapse. "Why I don't . . ." he stammered, "the books aren't kept here . . . it will take two or three days, maybe a week . . ."

"Five years in prison for keeping Indian Agency books anywhere but at the agency office." Trace didn't raise his voice but the words pierced deep.

"Maybe I accidentally left them in the back

room . . . yeah, that's it, give me a minute."

"Sixty seconds. One, two . . ."

In fifty-five seconds Klungbottom rushed from the back room, dumped four large ledgers of account sprawling on the table, and collapsed breathless onto a chair. "There's the books. I didn't keep those accounts. I don't know where those figures . . ."

"Five years in Leavenworth for the agent not keeping the books."

"Maybe I did keep them!" Klungbottom wailed.

"Sit right there," Trace said, pointing to a chair against the wall. "Don't move while I examine these books."

Klungbottom sat down, but never quit moving. His legs, feet, hands, arms, head, and body took turns at twisting and turning while he moaned and groaned, mumbling incoherent half-sentences while Trace opened the ledgers one at a time and ran a finger slowly down the margin on each page, head tipped forward, eyes narrowed.

An hour later Injun Charlie slowly approached Trace, keeping his body between Trace and Klungbottom. He leaned over and quietly whispered, "You got bad eyes. Can't read. What you doing?"

Trace nodded firmly and said aloud, "You're right, Cochise. Klungbottom is going to get at least sixty years in the Leavenworth penitentiary. Watch him while I finish. Shouldn't be more than another two hours."

Injun Charlie straightened majestically and faced Klungbottom. "Make one move, white man, Cochise eat your liver."

Klungbottom gasped and slumped backwards in

a dead faint. Injun Charlie caught him and propped him onto his chair, then resumed his place by the door. "Sorry, Trace. No mean to scare him so bad."

"Eat his *liver!*" Trace said. "Where did you learn to do things like that?"

"No learn. Make it up just now."

Trace shook his head and again buried his face in the books, not knowing when Klungbottom would awaken. Half an hour later Klungbottom groaned and began to mumble about liver and Leavenworth. Trace paid no attention, but continued his deep concentration on the books, going over each blurry entry.

At two o'clock in the afternoon Klungbottom moaned, "I got to go to the outhouse, bad."

"You sit there and hold it," Charlie said, frowning. "White man teach Indian to hold it, now it Indian turn to teach white man." He flashed one of his rare, wry grins.

Teeth gritted in pain, Klungbottom sweated twenty more minutes before Trace finally closed the last ledger and stood.

"I'll be back in two days with a written court order to pick up those books. I'd take them now but the law says they can't be taken out of the agency office without a proper order. These are going to the United States District Court in Boise. So I'll be back here in forty-eight hours. If the books aren't here, I'll arrest you, and it's my duty to tell you the penalty for removing these books or destroying them or altering them is fifty years to life in a federal penitentiary. If you or these books aren't here when I get back, there is no place on this continent that Cochise and his

Apaches won't find you. The only question is, after they catch you, can I get there fast enough to keep you from being scalped, your liver cut out and eaten while you watch, and your remains chopped into stew. Do you think you have some idea of what I'm trying to tell you?"

Klungbottom's eyes were fairly popping out of his head, the pupils black pinpoints. He was white with terror. His hair stood on end, and there was no muscle in his body that was not quivering. He moved his mouth to speak but no sound came. He jerked his head up and down twice to signal his understanding.

"All right. Two days. Ten o'clock in the morning. Be here."

Trace turned without another word and started towards the blurry wall where he remembered the door, and Injun Charlie quickly opened it so he could see the shaft of light. Injun Charlie fell in behind him and closed the door. Forty yards later Injun Charlie said quietly, "Wait. See if Klungbottom makes it."

The door burst open and Klungbottom fairly flew towards the outhouse, seventy-five feet distant. At the fifty-foot mark he slowed and began to walk with his feet thrown wide apart.

"Nope. Him lose race." They both grinned. As they walked on Injun Charlie said, "You feed Klung-bottom lies. Me not Cochise. You not get order for books. No eat his liver. No cut him into stew. Where you learn to lie like that?"

Trace turned his face to Injun Charlie. "From an old Indian friend of mine."

Injun Charlie smiled. A quarter mile down the

trail Trace stopped and held his finger to his lips for silence while he listened. "If Klungbottom wanted to make a run for the river on a horse, and get on over to Lumley's place, which way would he take?"

Injun Charlie looked north, then south. "Old wagon road. Half mile north. Road little longer, but he no be seen."

"Let's go. Take me there quick."

Ten minutes later they were crouched behind a windfall tree fifty yards from the old wagon road, listening intently. A minute passed before the distant sound of drumming horse hooves reached them and quickly grew louder. Around the bend came Klungbottom, wildly kicking a gray horse in the ribs, coattails flying, hat gone, hair streaming. The horse had its neck stretched far and low, ears laid back, mane flying as its blurred hooves threw dirt at every stride in its thundering stampede gait. A burlap bean sack was slung over Klungbottom's shoulder with four heavy objects the size of the ledgers inside, bouncing all over Klungbottom's back and the horse's hind quarters. Klungbottom shrieked, "Giddap, move, giddap," to the horse while his heels pounded its ribs.

Trace and Injun Charlie jerked their heads from left to right as the gray streak swept past them and was gone.

"Did he have the books?" Trace asked intently.

"Him have books."

"Considering speed and distance, when do you think Klungbottom will reach Lumley's place?"

"If he go whole way like he pass here, be at river in three minutes, horse jump river, be at Lumley place in two more minutes. If he go normal, eight mile to river, swim river, four more mile to Lumley. Maybe two hours."

"Good," Trace said. "Let's get back to the Settlement. We need to talk to Mole."

They set a steady pace, and Stump and the others were waiting for them when they strode into the Settlement.

"What happened with Klungbottom?" Kate asked.

For ten minutes Trace and Injun Charlie related the events of the morning. Then Trace turned to Mole.

"Could you make another trip over to Lumley's tonight?"

"Easy. Why I go?"

"Somewhere over there, probably inside Lumley's cabin, are four large, very important books, maybe this big." Trace demonstrated with his hands. "Heavy. Full of writing with a pen. Do you think you can get inside his cabin and find them without getting caught, and bring them back here without getting them wet or losing them?"

Mole beamed, "When it get dark."

"Good."

"Okay," Stump said, "that's settled. We got work to do on them wagons. Let's get at it."

In the golden afterglow of sunset, Stump and Gimp and Trace walked to the edge of the clearing to feed and water the sixteen mules. Injun Charlie watched them for a moment, then raised a hand to signal to the others to meet him on the other side of Kate's place. A moment later they all hunkered down near the back wall and Injun Charlie turned to Mole. "You still got keg of moonshine?"

"Keg still in log."

"Got big idea for Trace. Fix his eyes. Old Indian elixir cure."

Drinks Much puckered for a moment. "You think moonshine cure his eyes?"

Injun Charlie shrugged. "Don't know. No hurt to try."

Drinks Much raised his eyebrows and scratched his head. "Moonshine make Indian see double. Maybe make Trace see single."

Injun Charlie turned to Mole. "When I say, you fetch old clay cup full. Then you all do what I do."

They all nodded their understanding, then rose and joined the others for the usual evening chores They covered the sorted freight piles with canvas tarps, and staked them down. With supper and the dishes done, they all gathered around Kate's kitchen table for the usual talking over a cup of coffee, with Injun Charlie waiting for just the right moment.

"Trace," Injun Charlie said, "Injun Charlie cure your bad eyes. Make Good eyes. See close, see far, see everything."

Trace looked wistful. "I don't think so. I've been wearing glasses since I was ten years old. Doctors in Boston, New York, Washington, D.C.,—all over the east coast—have done all that could be done. I'll just have to wait until I get back there to get some more glasses before I'll be able to see again."

Injun Charlie frowned. "Not true. Injun Charlie know what wrong. Have ancient Indian elixir. Learn from great-grandfather when he eighty-one year old. Secret magic drink. Fix many thing. Fix eyes good."

Trace shook his head skeptically. "Your great-grandfather lived to be eighty-one?"

"No. One hundred eighteen. Teach me magic cure when he eighty-one."

Trace smiled. "You're making this all up. He never lived that long."

Injun Charlie shook his head emphatically. "Injun Charlie tell truth. He live hundred eighteen because he drink much magic elixir. You drink, eyes get perfect."

Trace put his coffee cup down. "I don't think so, but thanks anyway. It's about time to go to bed." He rose.

Stump put his hand on Trace's arm. "Better sit down and listen. I seen many a strange thing done by these Indians. Their medicine man saved my life once by putting a magic charm on me after I got bit by a rattlesnake."

Trace sobered. "You serious?"

"I'm just sayin', you might be smart to listen. Can't hurt. Might help."

"Mole fetch big snort," Injun Charlie said, and Mole instantly disappeared out the door. In ten seconds he was back with an old, chipped, battered clay Indian jar. The painting on the sides had long since faded and mostly disappeared. Inside was a pint of clear liquid. Silence gripped the room as Mole set the misshapen old jar in the center of the table and backed away from it with a sense of reverence.

Injun Charlie faced the vessel and the other

three Indians did the same. Injun Charlie placed the palms of his hands together before his face and slowly bowed his head in an attitude of prayer. The others did the same.

"Faderen. Nah-teesh. Shum-powie," he murmured. The other Indians repeated it.

Injun Charlie glanced at Trace and whispered, "Great Spirit must purify magic elixir."

Kate sat wide-eyed, transfixed. Stump was following every move, every word. Gimp sat in the corner, noncommital.

Injun Charlie raised his face towards the ceiling, clenched both fists before his eyes, and the other Indians did the same.

"Mana Kon-stet." He paused, then spoke louder. "Yus-tah. Toto. Kah-poof."

Mole opened his eyes a slit and glanced at Drinks Much inquiringly. Drinks Much glanced back at him, nose and forehead wrinkled, totally baffled. They both closed their eyes and repeated the words, with Lump faithfully mimicking them.

Injun Charlie quickly unclenched his fists and placed his palms over his closed eyes while the others did the same.

"Usen. Fix-um. Pronto."

The others repeated it.

Quickly Injun Charlie thrust his finger into the jar and stirred the liquid vigorously, then drew his finger out and thrust it into his mouth. He closed his eyes and savored his finger for several seconds.

"Magic strong. Fix eyes." He again tipped his head back, fixed his eyes on the ceiling one more time and loudly cried, "Hookahey."

He spun to face Trace. "Trace drink all magic elixir. Now."

Trace glanced at Stump, then Kate, confused and uncertain.

"Drink it," Stump exclaimed, and Kate nodded her approval.

Trace's face was a study of confusion and misgiving as he groped for the dim shape of the old jar, and fumbled for a moment while he found a way to grasp it. He wrapped both trembling hands around it and raised it to his lips, then hesitated.

"Hold your breath and take 'er straight, in one shot," Stump commanded. "Do it now, because the magic goes away if you wait too long. Do it!"

Trace set his jaw and his face became a mask of determination. He raised the ancient jar and tipped his head back and swallowed until the jar was empty. His breath left him for half a minute while the fire hit the bottom of his stomach, started back up, then settled. His eyes bugged and the pupils disappeared. Sweat sprouted on his upper lip, and rolled from his forehead. His lips formed a fine "oooo" while he tried to suck in air to kill the fire, but he could not inhale. The burning glow spread from his stomach to his chest, then his legs and arms, then his head. His face went blood red, then blue, from lack of breath, and as strange images began to dance before his eyes, he finally sucked in a great draft. His frame jerked straight and he slowly set the jar back on the table. Then he sat bolt upright, his face set as though in death, and he slowly tipped backwards off the bench, unconscious.

Stump caught him and carefully laid him on the

floor. "He's gone until morning. I hope this works, because he's sure gonna be mad if it don't."

Injun Charlie looked concerned. "Me hope it work too."

"Wait a minute," Kate exclaimed, fear creeping into her voice. "You ever worked this magic before?"

Injun Charlie shook his head and refused to look at her.

"What was that stuff, anyway?" Stump asked. "It smelled like straight moonshine."

Injun Charlie shrugged and looked humble. "Moonshine make good eyes blind. So Injun Charlie figure it make blind eyes good. Hope it works. In morning we find out if old magic Indian elixir work."

The blue jay tipped its head upwards in the fresh, clean, clear, mountain stillness and chortled his raucous greeting to the first golden beams of the rising sun.

"Oooohhhhhhh," Trace groaned, and clapped both hands over his ears while trip-hammers pounded inside his head. His tongue felt like a board with fur on it, and his mouth tasted like a late season backwater. For a moment he was certain no human being could survive the torments that had crushed him.

Again the blue jay set up his joyous salutation, and Trace writhed as he groaned and clapped his hands over his ears. In pain he opened one squinted eye, probing for the source of his tormentor, perched on an emerald-green pine bough nearby. The blue jay cocked its head to one side and ripped loose once more.

"Do it again and I get the shotgun," Trace breathed. He gritted his teeth and wondered if he could walk from beneath the wagon to Kate's door to get the weapon. He watched through his slitted eye as the blue jay dropped from the limb to the ground and came hopping towards him, head cocked in puzzlement at the huge mound of mumbling blankets.

"Quit stomping or you're dead," Trace breathed, and tried again to swallow the ball of cotton and fur in his mouth. He jerked at the sound of Injun Charlie's voice, and saw him rise from his haunches by the giant rear wheel of the wagon. Charlie grinned from ear to ear.

"What're you grinning about, you murderous heathen," Trace moaned. "You and your secret Indian elixir! Hah!"

"Here, catch," Injun Charlie said, and tossed a pine cone.

Trace caught it with one hand and dropped it beside his blankets. "I ought to make you drink about a gallon of that devil's brew," Trace lamented, and clenched his eyes shut at the incessant pounding inside his skull.

Injun Charlie stood and waved his arms at the others standing at Kate's door. They came trotting as Injun Charlie called, "Elixir work fine. Trace have eyes like eagle."

Trace froze. He blinked and fixed his gaze on Injun Charlie. For the first time he clearly saw every line, every crease, every detail of the two beady eyes and the hawk nose separating them. He sat bolt upright and watched the others approach. He gaped at the huge, round, grinning face of Lump, and the flat face of Drinks Much.

And for the first time he clearly saw Kate's auburn hair, green eyes, generous smiling mouth, and slightly turned-up nose, and his mouth fell open as he gaped, stunned by the natural beauty. Behind her stood Stump, a gigantic grin showing through his beard.

Trace threw his blankets aside and rose to his knees in his longjohns. He sprang to his feet, then dropped back to his knees, groaning through a grin. "I can *see!* Everything! Near and far!" He turned to Injun Charlie. "Bless you and your great great-grand-father for the secret elixir. Thank you. Thank you."

"Trace, welcome. Old Indidan elixir never fail." Injun Charlie drew and released a great sigh of relief.

"What is it made of?"

Injun Charlie glanced at Stump and Kate before he answered. "Secret. Tell later. Now you use good eyes to come for breakfast."

Trace rose to his feet and bit off another groan as his head throbbed. The ache was soon forgotten as he turned his head and saw for the first time the tops of the great, emerald-green pines blazing in the morning sunlight. He saw the striped chipmunks and bushy-tailed squirrels chattering and scurrying. At the far edge of the clearing, a doe deer and her fawn walked unafraid into the trees. Trace drew a great breath and stood for a moment in the full glory of a new world.

Suddenly his eyes popped and he glanced down, realizing he was in his underwear in front of Kate. "Kate," he stammered, "I'm sorry—I—didn't mean . . ." He grabbed his trousers beside his bedroll. Kate laughed heartily as she turned back towards the place. "Breakfast in five minutes," she said, and laughed again.

With everyone gathered around the breakfast table Trace hesitantly sipped at his coffee and waited to see if his stomach would accept it. It did, and he sipped again, and soon the ache in his head was gone.

"Pass the ham and eggs," he said, and while he filled his plate he asked, "Mole hasn't returned yet?"

"Not yet," Stump answered. "I'll give it another half hour and then I'm going over to find out what happened to him."

Kate listened for a moment, then walked to the door. "Won't be necessary. Here he comes with the books."

They cleared a place on the table and a few moments later Trace had the ledgers laid out and was quickly turning the pages. "I think they're all here," he said. "It'll take me about a day to piece this whole thing together." He closed the last ledger and looked at Mole. "Did you have any trouble? Did they see you?"

"No see me. No trouble."

"Where were the books?"

"In Lumley cabin under bed."

Trace raised an eyebrow in surprise. "Was Lumley there? How did you get in and out without being noticed?"

"Middle of night. Lumley snore like bull buffalo. Mole champion sneaker."

Trace grinned and shook his head. "The world champion," Trace said admiringly.

He turned to Stump. "What do you think Lumley will do when he finds these books gone?"

"I been thinkin' on that. By noon he'll know they're gone and two hours later he'll figger who got 'em. After he has a hissy fit he'll sit down and make a plan that includes gettin' these books back and runnin' you out of the country so you can't get him in trouble. So I expect him and his rowdies to pay us a visit. That's how I'm thinkin' about Lumley."

Trace glanced at Kate and Injun Charlie. Kate said, "Me too," and Injun Charlie gave one perfunctory nod of agreement.

"When? What kind of a visit? Could it get violent?"

"Probably scout us out in the early morning to be sure who's here, and come on into the place sometime after breakfast. Might get a little rough, and if one of them roughnecks has a pistol, who knows?"

Trace shook his head and put down his empty coffee mug. "I have a lot of pages to read and some heavy thinking to do. One thing is sure. It's a lot easier with eyes that work. Thank you again Injun Charlie."

Injun Charlie smiled and nodded.

Stump stood. "Come on, the rest of you yahoos," he exclaimed. "We got a lot of furs to tote down from the second floor and load into the wagons. Let's get crackin'."

At noon Kate set the table, interrupted Trace from his deep concentration in the books, and called in Stump and the crew from loading the wagons. They finished the meal and continued throughout the afternoon, Trace raising his head to look about from time to time to smile his delight at seeing the wondrous detail of a world that had been a dim blur.

At six o'clock Trace yawned and stretched and Kate set the table for supper. Kate said grace, and they all began passing the steaming bowls.

Trace paused. "Klungbottom's books show he signed receipts for twenty-four tons of grain over the past two years. If he did, and didn't give it to the Indians, then it must either still be there somewhere, or he has made a deal with Lumley to make moonshine. So, it looks like we need to have a talk with Klungbottom and Lumley together."

"Knowing Klungbottom, I doubt you'll get him to talk with you if Lumley's there too," Stump said. "That'll be tricky."

After supper they helped with the dishes and Stump got out the checkerboard. Trace walked out into the soft moonlight and silently circled the clearing, listening carefully. Satisfied, he returned to the cheerful light inside Kate's place.

"Kate," he asked, "where would be a good place to hide the books?"

"I've already done it. I wrapped them good and buried them in the flour barrel."

"Thanks."

Stump stood and stretched. "Trace, everything okay outside?"

"Fine."

"Think I'll turn in."

The men all walked out into the still night. "Stump," Trace said, "I think I'll bed down by the dynamite wagon tonight. If anything happens before morning, yell. I'll do the same."

"Good idea," Stump said. "Get a pick handle and keep it handy. I got one. You never know."

Stretched out in his blankets beside the great wagon, Trace let his eyes wander into the vastness of the black velvet dome, alive with unnumbered winking stars. A smile tugged as he realized he could see them, and count them. For a few minutes he counted, then grinned in the dimness. "Too many," he said quietly to himself. He let his thoughts reach into the vastness and he sobered, humbled with the realization of the smallness of the world and all that in it is. Slowly his eyes closed and he slept.

He was breathing deeply and never knew when the huge, lumbering shadow knelt by his side and peered down at him, then silently retreated to sit down and lean back against the rear wheel of the freight wagon with a blanket pulled tight about his massive shoulders.

In the beginnings of dawn, when the eastern sky had changed from black to deep purple and separated the heavens from the black rim of the earth, Trace's mind came from the far place of deep sleep to inquire, *"What was the moan?"*

It stopped, and his mind retreated to the warmth and comfort from whence it had ventured, only to be jolted violently. Trace jerked up in his blankets to a horrendous crash and the sound of a body flying through the boughs of a pine tree. For a split second his eyes opened wide as he peered into the velvety purple that for a few moments connects night to day. He grabbed the pick handle and threw his blankets back and sprang to his feet, poised, ready.

A panic-stricken shriek jerked his head around in time to see Lump hold one man by the throat with one hand, while he threw a second man head first against the side of the freight wagon with the other. Then he doubled up his free fist and the whomping thump could be heard for fifty feet as his fist whacked down on the second man's head. The man went limp and dropped in a heap.

A third man was backing away from the

monstrous hulk of Lump looming near the freight wagon, and the man spun and sprinted, not noticing Trace in his panic. Trace whacked him in the pit of the stomach with the pick handle and the man went down, rolling and gasping for breath. A second man followed, so terrified by the monster looming behind him that he didn't see Trace until the pick handle dropped him in his tracks.

In one huge stride Lump reached the last two men still on their feet and bear hugged them. Their pleading whines dwindled and died as their breathing stopped and they fainted, eyes bugged out, faces beet red. Lump released them and they sagged to the ground unconscious.

With daylight growing stronger every second, Trace quickly surveyed the battle scene and looked into the timber for others that may be skulking about. Nothing stirred. He heard running from behind and turned, pick handle ready.

"Hold on there, Trace, I'm Stump," came the shout. "The others are right behind me. What happened?" Stump was in his long johns, pick handle grasped firmly in his square fist.

"I think Lumley made his scouting visit," Trace said.

"How many?"

"Let's count them." He sorted them out. "There's six on the ground, Lumley among them. I recognize them from my visit at his place," Trace said. There ought to be one more somewhere—a blocky man with a pistol."

Gleefully, Lump pointed into the nearest pine. There, twenty feet above ground level, the seventh man was draped over a pine limb, unconscious.

"That's seven," said Stump. "Cuss the dang luck. I never got a single lick. Goldang it."

Trace looked closer at the men to be sure none of them were dead, then walked over to Lump. "Thank you. You did good."

Lump bowed his head shyly and grinned. "White man speak with forked tongue."

Trace smiled back at him and patted him on the shoulder as Kate came trotting from her place. "How did it start," she asked.

"I think they stumbled onto us here in the dark, and one of them stepped on Lump over by the wagon wheel. He threw that one clear up into the tree, and then cracked that plank in the side of the wagon with another one. Two of them were so terrified of him in the dark they didn't even see me and almost ran into me. I hit them with the pick handle. Lump hugged those last two into unconscious." Trace shook his head. "Only the Good Lord knows how glad I am he's on my side," he said. He dug two lumps of mule sugar from his pocket and gave it to Lump, who popped it in his mouth and smiled his pleasure.

"Well," said Stump, standing in his long johns, "where do we go from here?" He slipped his hand inside his trapdoor and scratched. "We ain't got no jail for these varmints."

Trace puckered his face and scratched his jaw in thought. "I got an idea. Let's wake them up and feed them breakfast. Let me talk to them. This might be interesting."

"Now hold on there," retorted Stump. "We

ought to run these skunks clean out of the country. You sure about feedin' 'em breakfast and talkin'?"

"I think so."

Injun Charlie interrupted. "While these men here, my name Cochise. You all understand?"

He held his serious expression until the laughter died, and then waited solemnly until each nodded agreement.

Groans from all seven men echoed off the walls inside Kate's place as Kate cracked eggs and plopped large rounds of sliced ham into two giant skillets on the old, black, wood-burning stove.

"Here, Mr. Lumley," Trace said, "take a drink of this cold water. It'll help get your eyes focused."

Moaning his protest, Lumley grimaced and sipped at the tin cup. "Where is the dirty, rotten, low-down varmint that bush-whacked us? Of all the mean, conniving, blackheartd . . ." he paused and looked furtively at Trace to see if he had drawn the conversation away from why he and his six hench-men were sneaking up on the trading post in the dark, in the first place.

"I'm sure sorry about that, Mr Lumley. That was me and my friend. In the dark we didn't know it was you. We're sorry. I hope there was no permanent damage done."

"Like to of kilt all of us," Lumley retorted sourly, trying to mask his relief.

"Well, maybe a good breakfast of Kate's ham and eggs and coffee will help."

Lumley quit massaging his aching head for a moment and looked about suspiciously. He surveyed his men, who were in various stages of recovering their bearings, and then looked at the others gathered in the room. When he saw Lump his eyes popped and a look of stark terror seized him. He jabbed a finger at Lump.

"That's him! That's the one! For no reason he whomped us and flang us around and tried to kill us. Shoot him! Stop him!"

"No need, Mr. Lumley," Trace said soothingly. "One of your men stepped on him in the dark, and Lump didn't know what it was.He's very sorry."

The aroma of frying ham and eggs and coffee brewing filled the room and crept into every man. Lumley raised his nose and sniffed. "Well, a man like that ought to be kept locked up. Er, uh, did you mention breakfast?" He licked his lips expectantly.

Trace glanced at Stump and smiled. "Yes."

All seven men instantly forgot their aches and woes while Kate filled platters and coffee mugs and set them on the table. Kate said grace, and the men fell into total silence as they shovelled the food into their mouths and noisily sucked at the mugs of steaming coffee.

"I'm glad you came over today, Mr. Lumley," Trace said. "Saves me a trip over to visit you. I need your help, yours and your men's."

Lumley slowed in his chewing and eyed Trace suspiciously. "You need *my* help? What for?"

"I was over at the Klungbottom Indian Agency two days ago, and I found out his books show about twenty-four tons of wheat is missing. It has to be around here somewhere."

Lumley chewed slowly for a few seconds while

his thoughts whirled. "Well, maybe it was just stole. You'll never find it."

"Probably not. But twenty-four tons is a lot of wheat. Somewhere, somebody saw it and knows what happened. I have full government authority to do whatever I have to to find it. I was coming over this morning to hire you and your men, regular government wage, to help."

Lumley chewed thoughtfully for several seconds while he pieced together an answer. "Well, I would like to help, but we already got more than we can do over on my place. One thing I can help with, though. That wheat ain't on my side of the river. No siree. If it was over there, I'd know it. At least I can save you searchin' over there."

"Oh," Trace said, looking dejected. "I hoped you could help us look for it. But thanks for the information, anyway. I'll tell Klungbottom about it when I see him this afternoon.

Lumley began to fidget, then forced himself to look casual. "You goin' to see him this afternoon?"

"Yes. I told him I'd be back with an order to pick up his agency books for safe keeping. Stealing government propertly like that wheat is about fifty years in the federal pentitentiary, and falsifying records is another ten." Trace shook his head sadly. "Well, too bad you can't help."

Trace stood. "I better get ready to go see Klungbottom. By the way, what did you have in mind when you came to visit us this morning?"

Lumley's face fell and he stammered, "Well, er, uh, you see, I figgered, uh, our pigs—yeah that's it—our pigs over there. They're big enough for market and I come to make a deal with Kate. A lot of people come to her place and I figgered I'd offer her a dollar for every pig she can sell, and five dollars for every mule. That's why I come over. But I can see with one eye she's got more to do than sell pigs, so I don't reckon it'll work. I'll be heading back. Come on, let's go." He stood and motioned to his crew as he started for the door.

Trace shot a look at Kate, and she read his expression, and quickly said, "Why, that's a good idea, Mr. Lumley. I accept your offer. One dollar for pigs, five for mules. How much are you asking for them?"

"No, uh, see, I never thought about how much fuss it's goin' to be to haul 'em acrost the river and all. It ain't goin' to work."

"For that price I'll come pick them up," Kate insisted. How much you charging for each?"

"Price! Oh! Well, that's another thing I hadn't thought much about. I don't reckon I'll . . ."

"It don't matter much," Kate said. "We'll sell 'em at whatever price you ask. You got a deal." She thrust out her hand to shake on it.

Lumley rubbed his sweaty palm on his pants leg. "I don't . . ."

Kate grasped his hand and shook it. "Now we got us a deal."

Lumley looked fierce. "No, we ain't got no deal!" he exclaimed. "I changed my mind before we shook. Too much fuss, crossin' the river and all."

Kate looked concerned. "No fuss, Mr. Lumley. We shook on it. You tryin' to back out of a hand-shook deal?" She looked shocked.

Trace said, "Looks like you got a deal, Mr. Lumley."

Slowly Lump rose to his feet and towered over Lumley.

Lumley backed up two hasty steps, gazing whitefaced at Lump. "Well, uh, I guess maybe it wouldn't hurt to try it a time or two to see if it works. Now I got to go." He licked dry lips and gave a gesture to his crew to follow and quickly strode out the door, fuming with frustration and anger.

Trace followed and walked beside him. "Don't worry too much about that missing wheat, Mr. Lumley. When I pick up those books from Klungbottom this afternoon, I think I'll just give him a government order to be here at Kate's place tomorrow, probably around two in the afternoon. After he spends a night thinking about spending fifty or sixty years in prison, I bet he'll remember a whole lot of things. So don't worry about the wheat. We'll find it. Thanks for coming over. Good luck with your pigs and mules."

Trace thrust both hands in his pockets and watched Lumley and his crew disappear into the timber towards the river. Then he walked thoughtfully back to Kate's place and sat down with the others while Kate served them their breakfast.

He looked at Injun Charlie. "Cochise, you ready to go with me to the Agency? I have to deliver a government order on Klungbottom to be here tomorrow at three o'clock in the afternoon to explain some missing wheat. I need a witness. Want to make the trip?"

"Cochise ready," Injun Charlie said, "but you say two o'clock to Lumley."

"That's right. I want Lumley here a little before Klungbottom."

Trace turned reflectively to Drinks Much. "How many Indians do you think you can have here by tomorrow at two in the afternoon, if you start now?"

"How many you need?"

"Maybe a hundred."

"What Indian do?"

"Just be here and act mean. Any of them know a war dance?"

"No. Blackfeet peaceful."

"Where can you get someone who knows an Indian war dance?"

"Mormon kids. Fort Lemhi."

"That's too far, and we don't have the time. Any of your Indians at least have a tom-tom or something?"

"No. Maybe make tom-tom out of empty moonshine keg."

"While we're gone, get the word out to them. Tell them to be here and bring their bows and arrows and tomahawks and feathers and war paint, along with their tom-toms."

"Nobody have bow and arrow and tomahawk. Blackfeet peaceful."

Trace shook his head. "Well, can you at least start them making some tom-toms?"

"How much pay?"

"What do you mean, pay?"

"Indian no come without pay."

"You mean we have to pay them?" Trace asked dubiously.

"White men teach Indian. No pay, no work. No

pay, do nothing. How much you pay Indian to come?"

"I don't know."

Instantly Drinks Much interrupted. "No worry about pay. "Indian get pay from moonshine at Lumley place. Plenty moonshine still there. For five barrel moonshine, have Indian here, stand around, do nothing. Ten barrel, Indian make bow and arrow, tom-tom too. Fifteen barrel, learn war dance, look fierce, get plenty mean. Want five-barrel, ten-barrel, or fifteen-barrel job?"

"Now wait a minute," Trace said defensively. "I can't give Indians moonshine. That's against the law. I want a fifteen-barrel job, but I can't pay you in moonshine. Besides, you said nobody knows a war dance."

"No worry. You not need to pay us. We steal it. We make up own war dance. I got one hundred Indian, do fifteen-barrel job."

Drinks Much bobbed his head once, and the deal was closed.

Trace started to protest, then shook his head in resignation. He spoke to the others. "The rest of you sit down here at the table. We have some heavy plans to make."

An hour later Trace rubbed weary eyes with the heels of his hands. "I guess that does it. I hope everybody remembers the plan." He turned to Injun Charlie. "Cochise, give me a few minutes to write the order for Klungbottom and the two statements we have to get and we'll go to the Agency."

T race eyed the groups of feathered Indians gathering in a ring about Kate's place, fifty yards out, and called to Lumley. "Better come right on in, Mr. Lumley." He held the door for them while they hurried inside.

"What is them savages doing?" Lumley said, white faced and wide eyed. "Why, they got war paint and bows and arrows and tomahawks and all such out there, and they look awful mean. They going to massacre us?" He nervously wiped his sleeve across his mouth and looked out a small window.

"I don't know," Trace said, peering out with Lumley. "We went looking for that grain, and when the Indians found out someone had stolen twenty-four tons of their wheat, they just started showing up around here earlier today with all those weapons. I hope this doesn't get ugly."

"You better send someone for the army at Fort Lemhi, pronto," Lumley's voice cracked as he spoke.

"I already did. Stump should be coming back with the cavalry soon."

Lumley turned and scanned the room. "You got anything in here to defend us with? Rifles?"

Kate said, "I have some behind the counter here,

if it comes to that. 'Course, if they all attack at once, well . . ."

Lumley blanched and then as if remembering why he came in the first place, he scanned the room again and stared at Trace. "I thought Klungbottom was going to be here. It's him I come to see. I want to know if he's the one who stole that wheat, so I'll know what to tell folks when they ask if it was me."

Trace looked surprised. "Has anyone accused you?"

"Not yet. But besides me, the only other person around here that has enough trade to do it, is Kate. I just don't want no one starting talk that will hurt my business when Kate and me start selling my hogs and mules."

"We'll just have to see what happens when Klungbottom gets here. Maybe the Indians scared him off. Kate, do those iron shutters out there still close?"

"I think so. Haven't tried to close them in years."

Trace posted himself by one of the windows. "You saved us some time by coming over, Mr. Lumley. I got your claim for the loss of the medicinal alcohol written up, ready for your signature. It shows you lost sixteen thousand dollars. It says you swear it under oath, which is required by law. If you want your money you'll have to read it and sign it."

Trace pointed to a paper on the table, then turned back to keep watch on the gathering of Indians.

Lumley's fingers shook slightly while he labored, reading the claim. He skimmed most of the details and got right to the bottom line, which he understood well enough. It said Gideon Lumley claims losses due to Indian vandalism of sixteen thousand dollars, and the U. S. government was responsible to keep the Indians from doing it. He picked up the quill pen and shakily signed his name with a huge flourish, then dropped the feathered quill back on the table.

"There. That's my claim," he said emphatically, and walked over to peer out the window with Trace, "Seen anything of Klungbottom?"

Trace shook his head sadly. "Not yet. I hope those Indians didn't take him captive, or maybe worse."

Lumley swallowed. "He better get here quick!"

Lumley paced back and forth for five more minutes before he walked to the door. "Klungbottom ain't coming," he announced, "I figger he got kilt by them savages. I'm heading back across the river while I still got a chance."

"Good idea," Trace said quickly. "Maybe one of us better go out there and see if you can get through if you sneak out the back of the building."

"I'll go," said Kate. "They won't pay much attention to a lone woman." She slipped out the front door and closed it behind her. Then she turned and quickly located Drinks Much out among the Indians, and he waved. She raised her apron and waved it rapidly three times.

Drinks Much nodded, turned, and pumped his arm three times. Instantly thirty tom-toms appeared from nowhere and began their ominous, throbbing beat. Then Kate ran quickly around the building where Trace and Lumley could see her, both leaving and returning. She burst into the room, breathless.

"They're at the back of the building, just like in front, all painted and with arrows and knives. I don't think you'll make it back there."

Drinks Much pumped his arm again and the sound of the tom-toms beat wildly against the walls of the battered old building, each tom-tom beating its own cadence, with none of them matching. Drinks Much screwed his face into a disgusted prune and muttered, "Dumb Indians." He ran forward until all the Indians could see him and raised his hands. The drumming stopped and silence settled. Then Drinks Much dropped his hands and every tom-tom banged once. He quickly raised and lowered his hands eight or ten more times, and the fifty whiskey-keg tom-toms banged on the downstroke. With the cadence established, Drinks Much ran back to his own tom-tom and picked up the beat. Seconds passed as the steady rhythm ground out the message to Lumley and his henchmen of the horrible massacre that was just minutes away.

Lumley bolted across the room to the window opposite, then back to the middle of the room. "We got enough people in here to fight if they attack?" he demanded. He quickly counted. "Wait a minute!" he exclaimed. "Where's that big Indian who attacked us yesterday, and those ugly friends of his? They're missing. What's going on here? Are they out there helping those heathens with their attack?"

"No, they are not," Trace answered. "Cochise and his Apaches are out there now, outnumbered, doing what they can to keep the Blackfeet from attacking. They're probably saving our lives right this very minute."

At that moment, to the west, Klungbottom topped the last rise and went white as a bedsheet. He pulled his horse to a dead stop and froze in the saddle. He turned his head from side to side, staring in disbelief, dead certain every Indian in the west was gathered in a ring around Kate's place, feathered, painted, armed, and pounding a tom-tom. The moment he could force his hands to work, he drew rein and began to turn his horse.

From nowhere a small, grinning Indian with jagged red and yellow lightning bolts painted down both cheeks and across his forehead blocked his path, raised his tomahawk, and said, "Going somewhere, white man?"

Klungbottom went into deep shock. He jerked straight in the saddle and his eyes stared dead ahead, pupils pinpoints. The color drained from his head and hands. His jaw locked, and every muscle in his body went rigid as cast iron.

Mole lowered his tomahawk and waited to see if Klungbottom was going to fall off his horse. When he didn't, Mole took the reins and led the horse on down through the ring of Indians, and pointed the horse at the front door of Kate's place. He smacked the horse on the hindquarters with the flat of his hand, and the animal calmly walked on down to the building and stopped at the front door.

"I think someone just rode up on horseback," Kate said. "Maybe it's Stump." She cautiously opened the front door. "No, it's Klungbottom." She gestured, and Trace came running.

Trace and Gimp darted out and picked the rigid body of Klungbottom off the gray horse and set him on his feet, which were still separated, as though he were yet sitting on the horse. They waited, but not a muscle moved. Instantly they picked him up and carried him in through the door and sat him straddle of a stool, where he continued to sit as though still on the horse. His eyes had not blinked, nor had he moved a single rigid muscle.

Kate studied him intently. "He's scared clear out of his wits. Here. Splash some cold water in his face."

Gimp hit his head with a full bucket of well water, and Klungbottom gasped, and his eyes came into focus. Every muscle in his body relaxed at the same instant, and he melted into a trembling heap on the floor. "Indians. Millions. Painted. Feathered. Hatchets." For several seconds he mumbled and trembled.

Trace knelt before him, grasped his coat lapels, and slapped him lightly on both cheeks. "Klungbottom, look at me. You're in Kate's place. You're all right. Look at me."

Klungbottom fastened his eyes on Trace's face, then looked around the room as though coming from a deep sleep. "How did I get here? I was swarmed by savages. Swords. Axes. Who brought me here?"

"Your horse," Trace replied. "You'll be all right. Now settle down."

Kate thrust a mug of hot coffee into his hands, and he gratefully sipped at it. How did I survive the Indians who swarmed over me?"

"I imagine your horse galloped right on through them," Kate answered.

Satisfied, Klungbottom continued to work at the hot coffee.

Lumley sat down at the table opposite him and waited until Klungbottom looked at him. Lumley gave him an evil, meaningful look that said, "Mention the missing wheat and you're dead." Klungbottom looked startled, then frightened, and then buried his face in his coffee mug.

Trace turned from the window and took a heavy breath before he sat down at the table. "It looks like the Indians are getting ready for something out there. Klungbottom, you were supposed to bring the agency books with you. Are they still on your horse?"

Lumley looked at Klungbottom fiercely, and Klungbottom began to whimper. "No. No. They were stolen. I don't know where they are. The day after you left, someone broke into the agency and stole them, along with flour and salt and sugar and tea. Had to be the same heathens that are out there now, ready to massacre us."

"You sure they got stolen?"

"Absolutely."

"You ready to sign a sworn affidavit that says they were stolen from your Agency the day after I was there?"

"Yes, yes. I'll sign it," whined Klungbottom, looking for any way to get out of the place alive.

"I'll write it." Two minutes later Trace handed the quill to Klungbottom. "Sign if it is the truth."

Klungbottom read it quickly, and hastily scratched his signature on the bottom line. "There. That ends the question about the books and the missing wheat. Now get me out of here."

"Not so fast," Trace said quietly. "Maybe that

ends the question of the missing wheat, and maybe it doesn't. Lumley, you have a special, secret hog and mule feed over there. Where did you get it?"

"That ain't none of your dang business!"

Trace dropped the envelope with the letter from President Harrison on the table. "It *is* my business. Where did you get it?" His eyes bored into Lumley.

"Why, well, uh, I, er, we got it from someone in the East. Yeah, that's it. From Dakota. North Dakota."

"Good. Write down his name and address." Trace shoved the quill and paper towards Lumley.

"I don't—it won't do—he's dead. Dead. Just after I paid him off I got a letter saying he was dead. The secret was mine."

"Where's the letter?"

"Why, it must be—I don't know—at my cabin someplace. Maybe I threw it away. Don't mean nothin' anyway, except I own the secret feed."

Trace turned towards Klungbottom. "You got any idea about his secret hog feed? Where it came from?"

Klungbottom was livid, eyes jerking between Trace and Lumley. "Secret hog feed? What secret hog feed? I don't know anything about secret hog feed."

Kate spoke from the window. "Things are getting hot out there. They're stringing up their bows and whetting the edges on their scalping knives and hatchets."

Lumley's six men started towards the counter to find the rifles and ammunition.

Trace shook his head sadly. "Those Indians

117

believe Klungbottom and Lumley made a deal on the wheat. Poor heathens. They think the secret hog feed is nothing more than sour whiskey mash from making moonshine. If they attack, the only two people they'll want to massacre are Lumley and Klungbottom."

Klungbottom leaped and ran to the window. Outside, all the Indians were busy stringing their bows, checking their arrows, and licking their index fingers before gently running them down the cutting edge of their knives and tomahawks.

"I reckon we better get the rifles out," Trace declared. "We can't just turn Lumley and Klungbottom over to the Indians to be tortured and scalped and then chopped into stew meat, now, can we?"

Trace glanced at Lumley's six henchmen, who licked their lips and shifted their weight from one foot to the other, and nervously wiped at their dry mouths with their shirt sleeves.

"Kate," Trace exclaimed, "I'm going to make a quick circle around the building to close the battle shutters. You pass out the rifles and get ready. If I don't make it back, you men sell your lives to save Kate. If they fail, Kate, you keep one bullet in the pistol for yourself. Do you understand?"

Kate let her eyes drop and said bravely, "I understand."

Trace opened the door a crack, paused to peer out for a moment, then exclaimed loudly, "Now," and darted out. Kate slammed the door and dropped the bar. Trace circled the building clanging the huge sheet-iron shutters closed and dropping the cross bars to hold them. As he rounded the last corner he waved to Drinks Much and nodded vigorously. Drinks Much waved back and grinned from ear to ear before he waved to his men and they started down the slight incline to Kate's place.

Trace banged on the door, Kate jerked the door open for a second, and Trace fell into the room, panting heavily. He sprang back to his feet and slammed the huge bar across the door. "Almost got me. They're just outside. I thought that last arrow had me for sure."

With the battle shutters closed, the room was plunged into flickering lamplight, lending an eerie, unearthly pallor to the room.

"You men better get to the windows and bar those battle shutters from the inside. If they get them open, well . . ." his voice trailed off.

Something whanged off one battle shutter, then another, then all of them were banging and clanging. "Arrows and tomahawks!" Trace shouted. "They're making a full attack. Quick. Turn over the tables and make a barricade in the middle of the . . ."

"No, no!" cried Lumley's bald-headed henchman. "It ain't us they want, it's Lumley and Klungbottom. They're the ones what done it! They made the deal and stole the wheat." He darted towards the front door and started to raise the bar. "Throw them out. Let the Indians have them."

"Yeah, they're the ones," barked the bearded man who carried the pistol. "They're the ones should get massacred. I didn't hire on to get kilt by a bunch of barbarians."

Trace jammed the bar back into the brackets and shoved the bald-headed man back. "What? You mean Lumley and Klungbottom *did* make a deal and steal the wheat? What did they do with it?"

"Moonshine! Moonshine, you fool," howled the bald-headed man. "Now open the door." He grabbed Klungbottom and started towards the door, and Klungbottom sagged to his knees in a near faint.

"You mean the medicinal alcohol was just *moonshine?*" Trace said, eyes wide in disbelief.

"You *dimwit! Of course* it was moonshine. The hog feed over there is the sour mash from the moonshine stills."

"*What* moonshine stills?"

"The ones hid in the trees on Lumley's place. Open that door!"

The bearded man grabbed Lumley, who started swinging, and two other henchmen grabbed hold of his arms, and they wrestled both him and Klungbottom towards the door. They shoved Trace to one side and were working with the huge oak bar when Kate shouted, "Wait! I think they're right at the door. Don't open it!"

"Open it," bellowed the bald-headed man, and suddenly Klungbottom came to life.

"It was all Lumley's doing," he wailed. "He's the one that came to me and said we could be rich. Make moonshine from the wheat and feed the mash to hogs and mules. We could make a fortune off the Indians and pioneers. He done it."

"You fool," screamed Lumley. "It was *you* done it. Your big talk about having control of all that government property, and you could make us rich and no one would know the difference. It was *you* done it."

"Is there still moonshine over at Lumley's

place?" Trace demanded, standing before the door to block it.

"You dang idiot, of course there is," screeched the bald-headed man. "Dozens of barrels of it. Now move from that door or I'll whack you with a pick handle."

"Klungbottom," Trace said, "what was the deal? Who got how much money?"

"Half and half. Half to me, half to Lumley."

"Wait," Kate broke in breathlessly. "Listen. Something's happening outside."

The room fell silent in desperate hope. Suddenly Kate lifted the bar to the front door and jerked it partially open, held it for two seconds, then slammed it shut.

Outside, Drinks Much watched. "That's the signal," he said, and waved to his Indians. They quit throwing rocks at the iron shutters and retreated back to the fringes of the timber. He turned to the Indian next to him and nodded, smiling. The Indian raised an army bugle to his lips and blew the U. S. Cavalry charge, three times.

"Glory be," shouted Kate. "Stump got through. The cavalry is here. God bless Stump. He made it. We're saved."

On the bugle signal, the Indians quickly gathered up their tom-toms and bows and arrows and tomahawks, and in less than a minute they had all disappeared into the timber. One minute later Kate cocked her head at the sound of drumming horse hooves, and threw open the door.

Across the clearing, coming at the charge, led by Colonel Pape with Stump beside him, was a company of U. S. Cavalry from Fort Lemhi, their colors whipping in the wind, their guidons flying. Stump was riding old Tulip, kicking her in the ribs to keep up.

The big, stocky cavalry mounts swept across the clearing, and Colonel Pape pumped his arm three times. The troopers hauled in their reins and the horses set back on their haunches in a sliding stop. The soldiers, dressed in their campaign blue-black uniforms with the yellow stripes, looked glorious sitting at attention in the full sunshine, the dust from their skidding arrival swirling.

"You all stay here," Trace commanded. "You come outside and I'll have the cavalry and Cochise and his Apaches all over you. Understand?"

Klungbottom and Lumley and his six men all cursed and bellowed, but they stayed.

With Kate by his side, Trace walked out to meet the army.

Colonel Pape dismounted and gave them a smart salute. "The U.S. Cavalry at your command, according to your signal with the bugle. Do I understand you have a problem here?"

"Yes we do."

"Uh, er, it concerns a substantial amount of contraband that we're supposed to confiscate and dispose of?"

"A whole lot of moonshine."

The colonel drew a deep breath of relief and beamed from ear to ear. "I was a little worried there. We passed a few Indians coming in who waved and called greetings to us, and I thought we might just be asked to help with a few friendly Indians. Now where's this moonshine? Er, contraband?"

"Four miles past the river. Why don't you let your men rest and water their mounts for a while, and I'll get an Indian who can show you where it is."

"That will be fine. We can cross the river yet today, and have the illegal stuff under our control by nightfall."

"Probably not. The ferry is upstream about eight miles. It'll probably take quite a few trips to move your men and their horses across . . ."

Pape shook his head violently. "Our duty is to seize that contraband as soon as possible. We'll swim the river right here, the moment you give us a guide." His words were clipped, his eyes snapping. A roar of approval rose from the troopers behind him.

"If you say so," Trace responded. "Dismount your company and get the horses watered. I'll find your guide."

While the horses took turns at the watering trough, Trace walked to the pines at the edge of the clearing.

Grinning from ear to ear, Mole suddenly popped out from behind a rock. "Did we do good?"

"Beautiful. Outstanding. Have you already got your fifteen barrels?"

"Hide fifteen barrels down by Hubbards. Divide it tonight."

"Good. You ready to take this company of cavalry over and show them where they can find the stills and the rest of the moonshine?"

"Yes. But must hurry so can be back before midnight. We divide all twenty barrel at midnight?"

"Twenty barrels? I thought the deal was fifteen."

Mole grinned. "Lump no count very good."

Trace hid his smile and walked back to Colonel Pape. "Colonel, this is Mole. He speaks fairly good English. He will guide you across the river to where the moonshine is hidden. Destroy the stills."

A far-away look of sadness crossed Pape's face for a split second. "Destroy them. Yes, of course. And we'll be sure to secure all the contraband. We leave the moment the horses are watered."

Trace turned to Stump. "You get along all right?"

"Just like we planned her. How about you?"

"You wouldn't believe it. We got full confessions out of everyone, right on schedule. Now we got to decide what to do with them. Come inside. Before you do, though, you open the battle shutters on that side. I'll take this side."

Injun Charlie and Lump helped them open the battle shutters, then followed them to the front door. "You two wait here until I call for you," Trace said. He and Stump opened the front door and entered.

They had no sooner walked into the room when Lumley demanded, "Are the Indians gone?"

"Yes."

Lumley heaved a mighty sigh of relief. "Out of my way. I'm going too."

"Not yet you aren't." Trace stepped directly in front of him. "You're under arrest for stealing government property, making a false claim for sixteen thousand dollars under oath, conspiracy to defraud the government, and making illegal moonshine."

He turned to Klungbottom. "You're under arrest for conspiracy with Lumley to do all those things, plus falisfying government records, swearing out a false statement that government records in your care have been stolen, and removing Agency records from the office of the Agency."

He waited for a moment, then turned to the six henchmen. "And you are all under arrest for conspiracy to do all the things these men are arrested for, plus building illegal whiskey stills and distilling illegal moonshine."

The dark-bearded man shifted his feet and looked belligerent. "You think you two are going to stop all eight of us?"

"If I have to," Trace said levelly, and reached for a pick handle. Stump grinned and hefted one and spit on his hands.

"Start for the door whenever you feel like it," Trace said.

The bald-headed man bolted first. Trace whacked him in the stomach with the pick handle and the man went down. The bearded man fished his pistol from his pants pocket, and Trace caught him over the crown of his head with the pick handle. The man went slack and dropped in a heap.

Kate shouted, "You be careful, Trace," and clapped both hands over her mouth, stunned as she watched how he handled himself.

A third man charged Trace from the side, and Trace caught him in the face with his elbow, then turned and hit him with his fist. The man staggered back against the wall and slid down, eyes blank. The fourth man made a move, and Stump whacked him on the side of the head with his pick handle and he sighed and went down.

No one else moved.

"Anybody else want to try for the door?" Trace said quietly.

The remaining men eyed those who were on the floor for a split second.

"No sir."

"Uh-uh."

Kate found her voice. "Trace, why, I didn't know . . ." Her voice trailed off while she stood staring at a Trace she never knew existed.

Lumley puffed up like a big bullfrog. "This ain't legal. You ain't no sheriff. You got no right."

Trace tapped his shirt pocket where the letter from President Harrison was folded. "The President of the United States disagrees with you," he said. "All right. If this ruckus is over, you stand right where you are. Stump, if one of them makes a move, whack 'em."

Stump grinned from ear to ear.

Trace walked to the door. "Cochise, come on in."

Injun Charlie entered, followed by Lump, who seemed to fill the entire door frame.

"Cochise," Trace said, "where are the rest of your warriors?"

"Chase cowardly Blackfeet all directions."

"Didn't the cavalry scare off the Indians?"

"Cochise and warriors have Blackfeet running before cavalry get here."

"When will your warriors return?"

"When Blackfeet gone far. They run fast, like bunny rabbits. My braves return maybe tonight."

Trace turned to Kate. "Where are those books?"

In a minute Kate had the books out of the flour barrel, lying on the table.

Klungbottom's eyes bugged.

"Those are the books you couldn't wait to get over to Lumley's the day I first visited you, Klung-bottom," Trace exclaimed. "The government could have probably proved its case out of those books, but there's no doubt about it now. With your confession, this is a closed case. The only thing I don't know yet is what to do with all of you."

"Turn 'em over to the army," Stump suggested.

"I don't think we'll get the army back over here for about three days," Trace said, smiling faintly. He paced for a minute before he faced the eight men.

"We're going to put you in the smokehouse. There's no lock on the door so you can go whenever you want. The only problem is, Lump's going to sleep against that door, and Cochise and his warriors are going to be camped right behind it in the timber. If you think you stand a chance, give it a try."

"In the *smokehouse*," yelled Lumley.

"Yes, It's empty. There's no fire."

"Empty or not, you ain't putting me in no smokehouse!"

Trace shrugged. "Lump, put them in the smoke-house."

Lump grinned and took one step.

"Where's the smokehouse?" Lumley asked.

They all watched while Lump led them out, counted them into the smokehouse, closed the door, and waited for them to settle down. Then he walked back to Kate's place.

"Ain't you afraid they'll try to get out without Lump there?" Stump asked.

"They don't know Lump's not there," Trace

answered. "They'll stay put. We need Lump here for a while."

They all walked in and took chairs around Kate's table. A moment later Kate smiled, then chuckled. Then she chuckled again, and broke into a laugh. Stump picked it up and a minute later they were all laughing uproariously, pointing, jabbing each other in the ribs, reliving bits and pieces of the wild events of the day. Slowly they brought themselves under control.

"Trace, you're a genius," Kate exclaimed. "I don't expect I'll ever forget these past few days, but mostly today. I never saw anybody take on a whole roomful of men the way you did. And I don't know where you got the plan, but it couldn't have worked better."

"We all helped with the plan," Trace answered. "And I swear, that's the most fun I ever had in my life!"

Stump roared with laughter. "Anything back in the big city that can beat that?"

"Not anything. Not ever."

Stump sobered and spoke as though he had been waiting for the opportunity. "Anybody ever tell you that if you go back to that big city, you'll be in the wrong place doin' the wrong thing?"

Trace faced Stump. "What do you mean?"

"Just when I get some hope for you, you come up with some dumb question that blows it all away. Look at yourself."

Trace dropped his eyes to look.

"Yer standin' straight a full six feet, not hunched over. Yer not wearin' glasses and can see pine needles at one hunnerd yards, and that piddly cough is gone. Yer clothes don't fit no more because workin' that bullwhip has spread yer shoulders, and eatin' Kate's cookin' has put twenty pounds on you. Yer brown as a pine knot and tougher'n bull hide and yer legs is like lodgepole pines. You ain't no mousy little zero no more, the way you squared off with those eight men and had three of 'em on the floor before the others give up. And you just outsmarted Lumley, the slickest skunk in these parts. You ain't never been so alive in yer whole life. Now you tell me. You think you belong back there in that city?"

Stump's eyes bored into Trace, who sat with his mouth agape, thunderstruck. The room was locked in total silence as Trace swallowed and continued to stare. Kate held her breath, hoping, waiting. Injun Charlie didn't move.

Trace broke the spell in a quiet, subdued voice. "I never thought about those things. I hadn't noticed all that, Stump."

"Well, you have now. You better think her over before you make a real monumental mistake."

Trace started in shocked silence for several more seconds before he shook his head to force his mind back to reality. "We've got to figure out how we're going to punish those eight men out in the smokehouse. I think my presidential authority gives me that power. Sit down, all of you. We're going to work this out."

They talked and gestured and planned for more than an hour before Trace nodded. "I think we've got it."

"Pure genius," Stump said.

"I'll get supper," Kate said. "You men do the evening chores."

Half an hour later they sat down at the table and were soon lost in venison and sweet potatoes. Finished, they helped Kate clear the table, and Trace walked quietly outside, deep in thought. With the moon rising over the west rim, he returned. "Stump, how many more days before we're ready for the trip back to Pocatello?"

"Two, maybe three. We got the furs more'n half loaded now, and the animals is in good shape."

Trace started for the door. "I think I'll bed down. It's been a long day."

Stump followed him into the warm quiet of the forest night, with the three-quarter moon lending gray and silver to everything.

"Trace, what I said in there, think it over. There'll be a lot of freightin' needed in the next few years around here. I could use a good partner. And there's coal in these mountains, and timber to build towns. You and me could be in the middle of it, if you've a mind to."

Trace stopped. "That's the finest offer anybody ever made to me. It means something. I'll think on it."

"You do that. See you in the mornin'."

With his blankets spread, Trace was tugging at his boots when a shadow suddenly appeared and hunkered down beside him. "Injun Charlie! You surprised me."

"Biggest surprise coming right now," Injun Charlie replied. "Stump say truth, but only half. Injun Charlie come tell you other half."

130

Trace settled back. "What other half?"

"You listen to Stump, you learn who Trace is, but only half. Other half, you listen to Injun Charlie. You about to do stupid thing. You no notice Kate."

"What? Kate?"

"You dumbest smart man Injun Charlie ever meet. You no see light in her eyes this afternoon when you whack bad men? You no see her face when Stump tell you? You no see her put on special dress for you tonight for supper? You no see how she look in dress, her hair and eyes in lantern light?"

"Well, I've noticed . . . Kate's a . . . woman."

"Kate rare woman. One in a lifetime. You let her go, you biggest fool on earth."

"Me? Me and Kate? She doesn't think about me that way."

"You prime grade idiot. You not notice if freight wagon run over you. You no let Kate go. Injun Charlie has spoken." Injun Charlie rose.

"Wait," Trace blurted. "What am I supposed to do? What do I say?"

"Dumb. White man talk everything to death. Just go to front door, knock, when she open it, take her by hand, close door, take her out in moonlight, put arms around her, kiss her on kisser. No say nothing."

"Injun Charlie, you're crazy."

"No, you crazy one if you no do." Injun Charlie turned on his heel and disappeared in the trees without a sound.

Trace sat motionless for five minutes, his thoughts spinning. Slowly he pulled his boots back on and stood and walked to Kate's front door.

Silently Stump and Injun Charlie crept to the side of the building and slipped to the corner to watch.

Trace straightened, drew a deep, resolute breath, and rapped on the door. Kate opened it, he gently took her by the hand, and wordlessly closed the door behind her and walked her into the soft moonlight.

O rville Peabody hit the spittoon beside President Harrison's desk. "Boss, you fergot? Trace's here to report on that Injun rebellion, like you asked."

"Trace? Who's Trace?"

"Caleb Dinwoody."

"Oh! Him! He's too late. I've already sent General Nelson and half the army out to take care of that problem."

"Boss, there wasn't no rebellion. You better listen to Trace."

"I'll listen, but there's no calling General Nelson back."

"Don't drive them pegs too deep. Rootin' 'em out could be kinda nasty."

Peabody slouched over to the door to the oval office and swung it open. "Come on in, Trace. I reckon you already met the President."

Harrison stood with his grand, political smile. Trace entered, and Harrison's head jerked forward and his jaw dropped. "*You're* Caleb Dinwoody? You're supposed to be a mousy little . . ." he caught himself too late. "What I mean is, you're supposed to be an entirely different man."

Trace smiled and shook the President's hand. "I'm here to report to you, as directed."

"By all means. Sit down, sit down. But I must say, we thought those savages had killed you. General Nelson is on his way out there now with half the army to avenge you and stop the rebellion."

"There is no rebellion. Sending the army is the most comical mistake in the history of the White House. The citizens will probably march on Washington if they find out the truth about it."

"What truth?"

"The facts are in my report."

"What report?"

"You got a copy of it yesterday, from the Bureau of Indian Affairs. A copy was sent to General Nelson, as well."

"Where's my copy?"

Trace glanced at the stack of paperwork on the desk. "I think it's right there, near the top of that stack."

"Why didn't someone tell me?"

"No matter. I'll give you the brief facts."

For three minutes Trace spoke, using words sparingly, while President Harrison's eyes grew larger and larger.

"So we've caught Lumley and his henchmen, and they're being punished."

"You did all that *alone?*"

"No sir. Four Blackfoot Indians and a mule skinner and his assistant, and a woman named Kate, and a whole lot of their friends did it. I just helped."

"You mean the Blackfeet helped *stop* the moonshine trade?"

"Yes. Without those Indians, sixteen thousand gallons of raw moonshine would have been sold all over the territory at illegal prices, and would have caused more trouble than I care to imagine. As it was, those four Indians provided the West with the biggest show and best celebration ever known."

"The Indians did *that?*"

"Them and the cavalry."

"The cavalry got involved?"

"Colonel Pape played a big part in it."

"Where is the cavalry right now?"

"At Fort Lemhi, getting rid of the last eighteen hundred gallons of confiscated moonshine they seized before they smashed the whiskey stills."

"Are they burning it?"

"I don't think so. I never asked, but I understand morale at the Fort has never been higher."

"What punishment are you imposing on Lumley and his motley crew?"

"All of them are at Lumley's place, under guard, finishing feeding and selling three hundred hogs and one hundred mules for market."

"Under what guard? The army?"

"No. Two Indians."

"Two Indians? In heaven's name, who?"

"Lump and Cochise."

"Cochise! He's dead."

"Not the one guarding those eight renegades."

"Lump?"

"Just an Indian who can pick up the back end of a loaded freight wagon. Seven feet tall, about four hundred pounds."

Harrison's head was swimming with the story. "Is that the only punishment for those hoodlums?"

"Oh, no. They get to plow and plant and raise

twenty-four tons of wheat and deliver it to the Indian Agency in the next two years, to go to the Indians, along with all the money from selling the hogs and mules."

"And if they refuse?"

"We turn Lump and Cochise and their Indians loose on them."

Harrison shook his head in wonderment, then smiled. "Who figured all this out?"

"The bunch of us back there."

"Why Dinwoody, or Trace, or whatever your name is, that's genius."

"No, just good sense. The details, along with the signed confessions are in that report. I think that about finishes it." Trace turned to go.

"Wait a minute," Harrison exclaimed. "I already have the army on the troop train headed for the Snake River. What am I going to do about that?"

"Well, I guess you better get someone to work on the telegraph key and stop them. They show up out there and they'll be the laughing stock of the country, trying to stop a rebellion that never existed."

"But I had it put in all the newspapers! Army out to save the West!"

"If you want the army to save the West, send your generals out with orders to sit down with folks like Stump and Kate and Lump and Injun Charlie. They've got the answers. It's been a pleasure, Mr. President. Good-bye." Trace walked towards the door, his stride firm and strong.

"Wait," cried Harrison. "We might need you to explain some of this in person. Don't leave your office at the Bureau until further notice."

"Sorry, it's too late. I've resigned. I leave on the 7:40 train tonight. I've got a partner out there in the freight business, and there's a woman I have to see." He closed the door as he passed into the outer office.

Peabody greeted him. "Hold on for about a minute, Trace," he said, and walked into the oval office.

"Boss, you got a step ahead of yourself sendin' that army out there, and I doubt you're goin' to get out of it. If you stop Nelson you're a laughing stock and if you don't you're a fool. Either way, the newspapers are going to have a field day with you, and I doubt you'll survive the election."

"I know, I know," Harrison said in near panic. "What am I to do?"

"Well, judgin' from what that trip West did for Trace, I got a suggestion."

"Yes, yes, what is it?" Harrison asked eagerly.

"After you lose the election, go west and get a job muleskinnin'. Stump and Lump and them guys out there might give you a whole new life."

"Preposterous! Ridiculous! Impudent!"

"Just a suggestion, Boss. Might not hurt puttin' out a few feelers pretty soon to see who might need an apprentice muleskinner about November."

"Unthinkable."

"That's fer you to decide. Oh. One more thing. I quit."

"You *what?*"

"I'm headin' back with Trace. I seen enough of this town to find out what I come for. I figger I can get a job with Trace or Stump. Been nice knowin' you." Peabody pulled off his bowtie as he slouched through the door and closed it.

Harrison stood beside the oval desk in total shock. For five minutes he stared vacantly at the closed door, his thoughts whirling. Then he walked to the door and called loudly down the hall, "Phoebe, get a pen and pad and come at once."

A severe woman in a full-length black dress entered and sat down silently, pad in one hand, pen in the other, waiting.

"Phoebe, get a message over to Marples at the Indian Bureau. The message is, 'Come to my office instantly and be prepared to discuss in detail all the facts needed to make the following determinations. 1) What is a muleskinner? 2) What are his duties? 3) How long does it take to acquire those skills?'"

About the Author

Ron Carter is a research and writing director for the Superior Court System of Los Angeles County, California. He received a bachelor's degree in industrial management from Brigham Young University and a juris doctor degree from the law schools at George Washington University and the University of Utah. He is the author of *Prelude to Glory, Volume 1: Our Sacred Honor; The Trial of Mary Lou;* and *The Royal Maccabees Rocky Mountain Salvation Company.*